KING

SHADOWRIDGE GUARDIANS MC

BOOK 11

KATE OLIVER

CONTENT WARNINGS

This book is a DD/lg romance. The MMC in this book is a Daddy Dom and the MFC identifies as a Little. This is an act of role-playing and/or a lifestyle dynamic between the characters and falls under the BDSM umbrella. This is a consensual power exchange relationship between adults. In this story there are spankings and discussions of other forms of discipline as well as heavy age play.

Please do not read this story if you find any of this to be disturbing or a trigger for you.

ONE
ELLA

Ella stepped into her new house with a breathless squeal, twirling in the center of the tiny living room. The scent of fresh paint and old wood filled the space. It was different from anything she'd experienced before, but it was perfect because it was hers, and she got to make it her own. The owner of her new home had been more than kind, telling her she could do anything she wanted to it, and she couldn't wait to do just that.

Shadowridge was smaller than the cities she had known, quieter, but to her it felt like the perfect blank slate, a fresh start wrapped in charm, kind people, and a future she'd always wanted. She'd always be thankful for growing up in New York, but while her parents loved living in the big city, she'd never thrived. It was too busy, too loud, too much of everything she hated. Thankfully, her parents, though they were worried about her moving so far away, supported her choice to try somewhere new. She knew some people weren't as lucky as she was.

She set her suitcase near the boxes that had been delivered yesterday, surveying her new home. It was cozy, barely big enough for the small loveseat tucked into the corner, a kitchenette with mismatched cabinets, and a bay window that let in a good amount of light and would be the perfect space for reading. The bedroom had just enough space for the twin bed, which she secretly loved because it would be the perfect kind of bed to make her feel extra Little, and the bathroom was compact but well thought out with built-in storage. Everything about the place was small, but she loved it instantly.

Humming to herself, she started to unpack. Her clothes, mostly soft, pastel sweaters and skirts, fit neatly into the narrow antique wardrobe. She lined her few pairs of shoes along the base, then turned to her favorite part of unpacking. Decorating.

One by one, she pulled out her treasures. A stuffed rabbit, its ears well-loved and floppy, took its place on her pillow. A delicate music box painted with roses, which her mom had given her, went on the nightstand. She draped frilly, lace-trimmed tapestries over the walls, transforming the plain space into a dreamscape of pinks and creams. Fairy lights came next, twinkling where she strung them above the window frame, over the cabinets in the kitchenette, and along a wall shelf in the living room. A girl could never have enough twinkly lights.

By the time she was done, the tiny house felt like hers. Warm, safe, and filled with all her favorite things. She'd check out some of the local thrift stores to find some more pillows for the window seat and a few other things to personalize the space a bit more.

Sighing happily, she flopped onto the bed, sinking into the plush comforter she had brought with her.

"Home," she whispered to the stuffie, giving its ear a gentle pat. "We did it. All on our own, Rabbit."

Her parents didn't understand her desire to live by her own means. They were rich, and Ella had always lived a privileged life, something she'd always be thankful for. But throughout her teenage years, going to private schools, and living the life that most people dreamed of, she had always wanted to know what it was like to be a regular person. Without drivers, without butlers, without money. Which is why she had refused to take a single dollar of her parents' money when she moved. If she was doing this, she was doing it on her own. They hadn't understood why, but at least they had respected her wishes. Part of her wondered if her parents felt proud of her because of what she wanted to do.

She sent them a text message, letting them know she was settled in and that she loved them, to which they promptly responded, saying they loved her as well and to keep in touch.

As the sky darkened outside, Ella spent some time figuring out what she would wear on her first day at work. Despite Shadowridge being a small town that wasn't overly fancy, she still wanted to impress her new boss. Working as the mayor's assistant, she was sure she would have eyes on her at times, and she wanted to represent him well. From all her research, the mayor was well-liked and respected. He was into helping the less fortunate and was working on a project to help people with mental health struggles find the resources they needed. While Ella didn't know a lot about politics, she knew enough to know there needed to be more politicians like Mayor Winslow in the world.

After finally deciding on an outfit, she showered and dried her hair, then put on her favorite pair of footie pajamas, the fabric soft and warm against her skin. She grabbed Rabbit and took him to the living room to sit with her in the window seat, which she'd decided was already her favorite spot in the house. Then she turned on her e-reader and got lost in the story she'd been reading for the past few days. It wasn't until she nearly dropped the device that she realized how sleepy she was, so she set it aside and went to her bedroom to get into bed.

Ella nestled under her blanket and reached for the pacifier she had tucked beneath her pillow, sliding it between her lips with a contented sigh.

Tomorrow, her new adventure would begin. With that final, happy thought, Ella drifted asleep, the soft glow of her fairy lights casting a dreamy haze over her new home.

TWO
KING

The low growl of engines echoed through the streets as King and his brothers rumbled toward the clubhouse. The air was crisp, carrying the familiar aroma of pine that seemed to be the official scent of Shadowridge. That and cotton candy if you were anywhere near Main Street. His fingers flexed on the grips of his Harley, the steady vibrations of the machine grounding him.

Storm rode beside him, his blacked-out bike gliding effortlessly over the asphalt. Kade and Doc followed closely behind, the four moving as one. They'd spent the last couple of hours riding the curves of the surrounding mountains, letting the road stretch ahead of them, the hum of their bikes the only conversation needed. It was a good ride. A necessary one.

The clubhouse came into view, the glow of the Shadowridge Guardians' emblem casting long shadows over the parking lot. As they rolled in, King caught sight of movement near the playground to the side of the clubhouse.

The Littles.

There were a handful of them, giggling and playing, their bright energy a stark contrast to the rough exterior of the MC.

The Guardians protected their own, and the Littles of the club were family. They softened the edges of all the men.

He swung off his bike, running a hand through his short, dark hair before striding over with his brothers. Kade was already chuckling as his Little, Remi, ran straight for him, her arms outstretched. Storm scooped up his girl, Brook, spinning her in the air before settling her on his hip, her delighted laughter filling the space. Storm had really gotten soft since he'd met Brook. The man had been closed off and grumpy as hell before her, but now, he looked like he was truly living.

King felt a pull on his hand. He looked down to find Molly, one of the newer Littles, gazing up at him with wide, hopeful eyes.

"King, will you push me on the swings, please?" she asked sweetly.

He huffed out a low chuckle. "Yeah, sweetheart. Let's go."

After leading her to the swings, he helped her settle on one before stepping behind her, giving a gentle push. She kicked her legs, giggling as she went higher, her gentle curls bouncing with every movement.

He watched her, a strange warmth settling in his chest. He enjoyed this, being here, looking out for Littles, making sure they felt safe. It was part of what being a Guardian meant. Faust was her Daddy, but King still loved being part of Molly's life. All the Littles' lives, actually.

But as he stood there, hands steady on the swing's chains, a tugging thought crept in, one that had been lingering in the back of his mind for longer than he cared to admit.

He wanted *this*. Not just to be the uncle who watched over his brothers' Littles, but to have one of his own. Someone to come home to. Someone to take care of.

With a final push, he let Molly soar into the air before catching the swing, slowing it down carefully. "All right, cute stuff. I gotta head inside."

Molly pouted slightly but nodded and gave him a brilliant smile. "Okay. Thank you for pushing me, King!"

He ruffled her hair lightly before making his way toward the clubhouse. The others were still by the playground, but he had to get ready for his shift. Firehouse duty didn't wait for anyone.

Inside his apartment, he peeled off his cut, hanging it on the hook by the door. After showering and packing his bag, he flipped off the lights and let out a sigh, the heavy thoughts from earlier still there.

Maybe one day.

Maybe soon.

With a quiet sigh, King grabbed his keys and headed out.

The morning sun beamed through the open bay doors of the firehouse, the air laced with the scent of diesel and freshly brewed coffee. King stood at the back of the engine, restocking the med kit and checking supplies. His gloved hands moved on autopilot, pulling out expired bandages and replacing them with fresh ones, making sure the trauma shears were where they should be. Organization saved lives in this line of work, and King wasn't the type to cut corners.

Across the bay, Jenkins and Moore bickered over whose turn it was to clean the kitchen, while Holt, the oldest and baldest man in the firehouse, leaned against the truck, sipping from a massive mug that proudly read *World's Sexiest Fireman*. It was just another morning at the station.

"All right, listen up." Captain Mendez's deep voice rang through the space as he stepped out of his office. Instantly, the casual chatter died down. The man had that effect. Grizzled, sharp-eyed, with a presence that commanded attention. He deserved it, though. The man would never ask his men to do anything he wouldn't, and King had always had immense respect for him because of that.

"The mayor's coming by later today," Mendez continued. "Bringing his new assistant. She'll be helping with the city food drive, so they're doing a walk-through to get a feel for the layout. She'll be working out of one of the empty offices here part of the time."

Ramos snorted. "Poor girl. Probably doesn't know what she's getting herself into being around a bunch of firemen."

Holt grinned. "Wonder if she'll take over cooking duty for me."

King barely paid attention to the back-and-forth. It didn't matter to him. She would be here to do a job just like he was. And while they guys were having fun talking crap now, King knew they'd be polite to the mayor's assistant once she was there. The crew liked to talk big and bad, but they were a group of truly good men. It's why he was proud to ride truck with all of them.

Hours later, when a sleek black town car pulled up outside the station and Mayor Winslow stepped out, followed by a petite woman with bright eyes and soft curls, King's heart damn near stopped.

She was beautiful. Not only that, she was adorable, too. He wasn't sure how she was both things at once, but she was.

Her outfit was professional, but there was something undeniably warm and soft about her. Her hair fell in waves around her shoulders, and if he hadn't been paying attention, he might have missed the small blue barrette tucked into it on one side of her part. Then there were the sparkly blue ballet flats she wore. Add in the blouse with bow-shaped buttons down the front and King could swear she was a Little.

And then she tripped.

It happened fast. One second, she was stepping out of the car; the next, her foot caught on the curb, and she went down with a startled squeak.

King was already moving.

She landed on her hands and knees, her expression a mix of embarrassment and mild horror. Before she could scramble to her feet, King crouched beside her.

"You okay?" His voice was steady as he scanned for any real injuries.

Her cheeks were flushed as she turned her scraped palm upward. "I, um… I meant to do that."

King huffed out a quiet chuckle. "Sure, you did."

She bit her lip, looking away. "I'm fine, really. Just… maybe a tiny bit mortified. Did everyone see? They did, didn't they? So embarrassing. Sheesh. You'd think I'd be able to walk in flats. Maybe I should have worn heels, then I would have been fine."

As she rambled, he couldn't take his eyes off her. She was so fucking cute. And funny.

"It's not a big deal. Just a small owwie," King assured her, already pulling an antiseptic wipe from his pocket. "Happens to the best of us."

Gently, he took her hand, running the cool wipe over the graze. She hissed at the sting but didn't pull away. Up close, she smelled like vanilla and brown sugar, something that didn't belong in a place filled with smoke, sweat, and grease.

"I appreciate the rescue," she murmured.

Then, as if remembering, she straightened her shoulders. "I'm Ella, by the way. Ella Carter."

King glanced up, meeting her gaze. Something in his chest tightened.

Ella.

He didn't know why, but the name settled over him like something familiar. Like something important.

He gave her palm one last careful swipe before nodding. "King."

"King?" Her brows lifted. "That's your name?"

"Yeah."

Her lips quirked up in a smile. "Strong name."

King felt the corner of his mouth twitch, but before he could respond, the mayor started introducing Ella to the rest of the firefighters.

King released Ella's hand, but the entire time the mayor spoke, he couldn't keep his eyes off her. Even when they disappeared into the firehouse, he couldn't stop thinking about her.

One thing he knew for sure was that he had no idea how he was going to work around Ella and be able to concentrate.

THREE
ELLA

E lla tried to focus as Mayor Winslow guided her through the firehouse, explaining where the food drive tables would go and how they would organize donations. She nodded at the right moments, took mental notes, and even managed to ask a few intelligent questions. But if she were honest, she only absorbed about half of what was being said.

The other half of her attention? Completely tangled up in thoughts of King.

The name suited him for some reason. He had a commanding presence. But it wasn't just his name that had left an impression. It was *everything*. The deep reassurance of his voice, the rough warmth of his hands as he cleaned her palm, the contrast of inked skin and a gentle touch.

She had never reacted to a man like that before.

Sure, she'd been attracted to men in passing, admired them just like she'd noticed them admiring her. But this? This was different.

This was a wildfire in her veins and heat between her legs.

King was intimidating in the kind of way that made her pulse flutter unpredictably. The tattoos that peeked out from beneath his sleeves, the sheer size of him. Tall, broad, powerful.

He was nothing like the polished men in pressed suits she was used to working with or that she'd grown up around. He was different, which she liked. It was the exact reason she'd moved to Shadowridge. To experience something new in her life. She just hadn't expected it to be a hot fireman who got her all flustered and fidgety.

And yet, it wasn't only physical attraction that had her mind spinning.

It was the way he'd taken care of her so effortlessly. He hadn't laughed when she tripped. He hadn't made her feel small or ridiculous. He had simply helped her, steady and unshaken, cleaning her wound like it was the most natural thing in the world while trying to reassure her that it wasn't a big deal. That had made her heart react in a way she wasn't sure she was ready to admit.

She stole another glance at King as they moved through the bay doors at the end of the tour.

He was standing near one of the engines, talking with a few of the other firefighters. The navy-blue fire department T-shirt stretched over his chest, his arms crossed over his broad torso, muscles flexing as he shifted. Compared to her, he was so big. The contrast made something warm and unfamiliar coil low in her stomach. Ella had been aroused before, but this was on a whole other level. She was pretty sure she was going to need to change her panties when she returned to the office. Too bad she didn't have a spare pair with her. At least the ladies' room at City Hall had a blow dryer in the cabinet. She may not be drying her hair with it, but it would definitely be useful.

She tore her gaze away quickly, hoping no one had noticed her staring.

The mayor gestured toward the car waiting out front, and Ella smiled, smoothing down the front of her dress.

All right, time to go. Stop thinking about tattooed firefighters and get back to work.

But just as she stepped toward the car, King moved. In a

blink, he was there, striding toward her with long, purposeful steps. Before she could even think to fumble with the handle, he pulled the door open.

His gaze flicked down to her feet, then back up, the hint of a smirk tugging at his lips. "Figured I'd make sure you didn't trip this time."

Ella's breath caught. The teasing warmth in his voice sent a fresh wave of heat to her cheeks and between her legs.

"I—thank you," she managed.

Brilliant.

He held out a hand, an unspoken offer. She hesitated for half a second, then placed her fingers in his palm. His grip was warm, steady, completely surrounding her uninjured hand as he helped her step into the car without incident.

She settled into her seat, her pulse still erratic as he shut the door behind her.

The car pulled away, and she exhaled slowly, willing her heartbeat to settle.

"Good man, that one," Mayor Winslow remarked, pulling her from her thoughts.

She turned her head, raising a brow. "King?"

The mayor grunted. "One of the best in Shadowridge. Reliable, solid, good in a crisis. Always willing to help anyone in need."

Ella bit her lip, unsure why that made her feel warm.

The mayor glanced at her with a knowing smile. "Pretty sure he's single, too."

Her stomach flipped.

She turned quickly toward the window, hiding the blush crawling up her neck.

She wasn't looking for anything. At least, she didn't think she was. Then again, being in King's presence for a short amount of time had her questioning all kinds of things.

Ella hummed softly as she bounced down the snack aisle, her white Converse squeaking against the polished tile. She glanced into her basket, satisfied with her haul. Gummy bears, a rainbow assortment of chips, sugary cereal, boxed macaroni, cupcakes, and a six-pack of root beer.

All the essentials.

Dressed in her favorite pink leggings and an oversized lime-green sweater, she felt extra cozy, her high ponytail swishing with each step. The bow tied neatly at the top of her head was the cherry on top. Shopping like this, picking out whatever looked good without worrying about anything else, was fun. She couldn't understand why her mother always hated grocery shopping. As an adult, you could literally buy anything you wanted, and nobody could say no.

As she rounded the corner, she nearly ran straight into a broad chest. One covered in navy-blue fabric, decorated with a firefighter's emblem.

King.

She stumbled backward, gripping her basket, her heart giving a traitorous little flutter.

He stood there in his uniform, sleeves pushed over his inked forearms, the radio clipped to his shoulder, a half-smirk playing at his lips. He wasn't alone. Two other firefighters from the station were tossing things into a cart nearby, but Ella only had eyes for him.

King's gaze flickered down to her basket. His smirk deepened.

"Where's the real food?" he asked.

Ella frowned, then glanced at her collection of sugar and carbs. "It's right here."

King huffed out a quiet chuckle, shaking his head. "No protein? No vegetables?"

She wrinkled her nose. "For your information, there is protein in cheese, and there is cheese in the macaroni. Also, I got potato chips, which are made of potatoes, and I'm pretty sure potatoes are considered vegetables. And sugar, well, sugar is made from canes, which you have to grow, and let's face it, if you have to grow it, it's a vegetable."

He folded his arms, studying her like she was some kind of strange, new discovery that he was intrigued by. "Uh-huh. And what're you eating for dinner?"

Ella blinked, then looked at her basket.

Good question.

She bit her lip, realizing she hadn't actually thought that far ahead. "Umm…"

His brows lifted, clearly waiting for an answer.

She shifted on her feet. "Mac and cheese."

King let out a low chuckle, and the sound did something ridiculous to her insides.

"Do you always shop like this?"

Ella hesitated, then shrugged. "I've never shopped before."

That made him pause. His expression flickered with what looked like a mix of curiosity and confusion, but before he could press her on it, his radio crackled to life.

"Station Twelve, we've got a structure fire on Oak Street. All available units respond."

King's jaw tightened.

"Gotta go," he said, already stepping back.

Ella nodded as he headed toward the exit with his crew.

But before he disappeared through the sliding doors, he looked back at her.

And smiled.

It wasn't just any smile. It was the kind that sent warmth curling through her stomach, made her knees feel weak, and had her forgetting how to think properly.

It was a good thing she'd already gotten all the groceries she needed for the day.

Ella settled into her temporary desk at the firehouse, smoothing out the stack of papers she had to copy before the afternoon meeting with all the department heads hosting the food drive in their buildings. It had been a whirlwind of a morning: emails, calls, and figuring out how to use the ancient filing system the station apparently still relied on. But despite the chaos, she loved being here.

The firehouse was a hub of energy, filled with the sounds of laughter, boots against tile and the constant hum of radio chatter. The people felt relatable and real. It was so different from New York, and she already knew she never wanted to go back. She had no idea if Shadowridge was going to be her permanent home, but she kind of hoped it would be. Everyone was so nice here.

She grabbed the stack of papers and made her way to the copy machine, humming to herself as she pressed the buttons and waited for the clunky machine to do its thing. Or take off into outer space. With the noises it was making, it was possible either could happen.

But when she returned to her desk, she stopped short.

Sitting neatly on top of her paperwork was a black plastic container, the kind used for meal prep, with a folded note tucked under it.

Curious, she picked it up, unfolding the paper.

I'll sleep better knowing you eat at least one healthy meal today. - King

Ella's stomach did a little flip.

She bit her lip as she lifted the lid, and the second she did, the most mouthwatering scent hit her. The meal inside looked delicious. Grilled chicken, seasoned rice, and a mix of perfectly roasted vegetables that didn't look at all icky like the ones her family's cook had always made. She blinked, stunned.

He had done this? For her? Why?

A warmth spread through her chest as she closed the container and pushed to her feet. She needed to find King.

After checking the usual places, the kitchen, the bay, the break room, she finally found him in the back lot, checking one of the smaller emergency response vehicles. He glanced up as she approached, straightening from where he'd been inspecting the gear in the back.

She held up the container. "King."

His lips quirked slightly. "Ella."

She huffed a little laugh. "You made me lunch."

"I made the *station* lunch, and it seemed like a good idea to make sure you had some nutrients." He shut the compartment door, leaning casually against the truck. "Can't have you living off gummy bears and macaroni and cheese."

She stared at him, her heart still doing that ridiculous fluttering thing.

"I don't know how to thank you," she admitted. "This was so thoughtful. Although I don't know why you have such a hatred for macaroni and cheese. It's like the superior cheesy food."

King chuckled, then tilted his head, eyes dark and steady as he held her gaze.

"You can thank me by eating lunch with me."

Ella blinked, her fingers tightening around the container.

Oh.

A rush of something warm went through her, but she found herself agreeing before she could even think to stop herself.

"Okay," she said softly.

King smirked, that slow, devastating curve of his lips that sent her stomach into free-fall.

"Good," he murmured. "Let's eat. I'm starving."

FOUR
KING

King hadn't expected to enjoy lunch this much.

Sitting across from Ella in the firehouse's break-room, watching her take her first bite of a meal he'd made, he felt something shift inside him. She made a sound of delight as she chewed, her eyes fluttering closed for a second before she swallowed.

"King." She sighed, placing a hand dramatically over her chest. "This is so good."

His lips twitched, barely hiding a smirk. "Yeah?"

She nodded enthusiastically, already taking another bite. "Like, ridiculously good. Are you sure you're a firefighter and not secretly a chef?"

He chuckled, shaking his head. "Nah. But between cooking here and at my motorcycle club, the Shadowridge Guardians, I figured I better learn how to make a few meals; otherwise, I'd have a bunch of whiny men on my case."

"Well, I'm impressed," she said between bites, looking completely at ease.

King wasn't sure why it made him feel so damn good to watch her enjoy something as simple as chicken, rice, and roasted vegetables, but it did. Ella was easy to talk to, easy to be around.

Dangerously easy.

After lunch, he went back to work, checking equipment, running drills with the guys, and handling paperwork in Mendez's office. But no matter what he did, his thoughts kept drifting back to Ella.

And maybe a little too conveniently, his feet did as well.

The first time, he'd told himself he was grabbing coffee and *happened* to pass her office.

The second time, he claimed he was checking the mail, though he was pretty sure Holt had given him a knowing look when he veered in Ella's direction instead.

The third time, he actually had an excuse. Mendez had sent him to grab some forms, but when he stepped into her office, he found Ella sitting at her desk, quietly petting a small, palm-sized plush stuffed animal.

She didn't notice him at first. Her fingers ran gently over the toy's soft fur, her expression relaxed and almost serene. But the second she spotted him in the doorway, she stiffened, her face flushing pink.

"Oh," she squeaked, quickly placing the stuffed toy down. "I —I didn't hear you."

King leaned against the doorframe, arms crossed. "You always carry that around?"

Her face went even redder. "I—I know it's silly," she mumbled, not meeting his gaze. "It just... helps with my anxiety."

King studied her for a second before shrugging. "Nothing silly about that."

Ella blinked, clearly surprised.

He gestured toward the plush toy. "If it helps, it helps."

Her fingers fiddled with the hem of her sleeve as she gave him a shy smile. "Thanks. I'm still getting used to being in a new place."

He let a beat of silence pass before asking, "Where're you from, anyway?"

"New York City."

"So, you picked up and moved for this job?"

She let out a soft laugh. "Pretty much."

"Brave."

Ella rolled her eyes. "Or reckless."

He smirked. "Same thing sometimes."

She tilted her head. "What about you? Have you always lived in Shadowridge?"

"Yeah," he admitted. "Born and raised. Working here, riding with the Guardians, it's home."

Ella perked up a little. "The Guardians? Oh, that's your motorcycle club, right?"

He nodded. "Yeah. Shadowridge Guardians. We look out for the town, run charity events, help out where we can."

"That's… cool," she said, sounding genuinely impressed.

King's smirk deepened. "We're having a BBQ at the club-house this weekend. You should come."

Ella blinked, caught off guard. "Oh. Uh…" She glanced down at her desk, then up at him again. "I don't know. I mean, I wouldn't really fit in there."

King raised a brow. "Why not?"

She gave him a small, sheepish look. "I don't exactly scream 'biker chick.'"

King let out a low chuckle. "Good. Wouldn't suit you." He pushed off the doorframe. "Just think about it."

Ella bit her lip. "Okay."

King smirked, picked up the forms he'd come in for, and grabbed one of her sticky notes to jot down the information. "Good. Here's the address. I hope to see you there."

The smell of sizzling meat and charcoal filled the air, mingling with laughter, music, and the occasional roar of an engine. The Guardians' clubhouse was alive with energy, the compound packed with MC members and their families. King stood by the grill, tongs in hand, flipping burgers while Steele and Faust bickered about the best way to season ribs.

King wasn't paying attention to their argument, though. Mostly because they had the same one every time the club had a BBQ, and neither of them could ever agree, so the ribs were usually overly seasoned but still good as hell. It was meat. Meat was always good.

His eyes kept drifting toward the parking lot, his pulse racing faster with each passing second. He told himself he wasn't waiting for her, but when a small car pulled in and parked up, his heart gave a sharp, unexpected jolt.

Then the door opened, and she stepped out.

Ella.

King exhaled slowly, something tightening in his chest. She looked like she'd stepped straight out of a dream. Soft, delicate, cute. Her dark hair was styled in two space buns, little curls framing her face. She wore a babydoll dress, short and flowy, with tiny white flowers scattered across the fabric. And on her feet—those same white Converse from the grocery store, slightly scuffed but still somehow fitting with her outfit.

And that was when it hit him.

She looked Little.

The way she dressed, especially out of work, the way she carried that stuffed toy in her office, the way she shopped like a kid left unsupervised with a credit card. It all clicked into place.

King had been around enough Littles at the clubhouse to recognize the signs. Some were more open about their lifestyle, some more subtle. But Ella? She was completely unaware of the energy she gave off, and that made her even more adorable.

He smirked to himself, shaking his head before pushing off the grill and making his way over to her.

As he approached, he noticed she had a bowl in her hands, clutching it carefully and scanning the crowd. When her gaze landed on him, her lips parted slightly, cheeks coloring the faintest shade of pink.

"Hey, you made it," King said, stopping in front of her.

Ella smiled, her fingers tightening around the plastic wrap on the bowl. "Yeah. Figured I'd at least make an appearance. If I'm going to be in town for a while, I should probably get to know some of the people."

He didn't like the sound of her saying 'for a while'. Was she not planning to stay in Shadowridge? That would suck. He'd just started getting to know her and he already wanted to learn so much more about sweet little Ella.

He glanced down at the bowl. "What's that?"

Her blush deepened, and she hesitated before peeling back the lid, revealing a chaotic mix of brightly colored sweets—gummy bears, M&Ms, licorice pieces, candy-coated chocolates, sour worms, and even tiny marshmallows.

King blinked several times, his stomach turning over at the thought of taking a bite of what was in that bowl. "…What am I looking at?"

Ella chewed her lip, suddenly looking unsure. "A candy salad."

He arched a brow, unsure he'd actually heard her correctly. "A what?"

She huffed a laugh, shaking her head. "Like a fruit salad. But, you know… with candy instead of fruit."

King let out a deep, rumbling chuckle, rubbing a hand over his jaw as he glanced back at the ridiculous concoction. "Jesus, dollface. I don't know whether to be impressed or concerned about your blood sugar levels."

Ella giggled, nudging him lightly with her elbow. "It's fun! You mix all your favorite candies together and boom. Instant sugar heaven."

King shook his head, smirking. "You really don't eat real food, do you?"

She gasped, mock-offended. "Excuse me, this *is* real food."

He chuckled again, reaching out and plucking a single gummy bear from the bowl. He popped it into his mouth, chewing thoughtfully before nodding. "All right. Not bad. But don't think this counts as a meal."

Ella giggled, pleased. "It's a *side dish*. If I were bringing the main meal, I would have brought something much healthier. Like a Jell-O salad."

King exhaled, looking down at her with a grin. She was trouble. Soft and sweet, the kind of trouble he hadn't known he wanted until now.

With a playful shake of his head, he hooked a thumb toward the grill. "Come on, let's get some real food before you go into a sugar coma."

Ella grinned, hugging her candy salad as she followed him toward the rest of the party.

And for the first time in a long time, King felt like maybe something in his world had shifted. Maybe it was his turn to find his one.

And he didn't mind it one bit.

FIVE

ELLA

Ella stayed close to King as he led her through the compound, introducing her to one Guardian after another. The men were as intimidating up close as they were from a distance. Broad, tattooed, rough around the edges. But despite their slightly terrifying exteriors, every single one of them greeted her warmly, some with smiles, others with nods of approval.

"This is Kade," King said, gesturing to a man with sharp eyes and shoulder length hair. His arms were heavily inked, and his cut had the word *Enforcer* stitched into the leather.

Kade grinned at her. "Welcome to the madhouse, sweetheart."

Before she could reply, a woman, dressed head to toe in all black, appeared at his side, slipping her hand into his.

"This is Remi," King added, gesturing toward her.

Ella smiled. "Hi, it's nice to meet you."

Remi's eyes lit up. "It's nice to meet you, too! I love your dress!"

Ella flushed slightly, glancing down at herself. She was surprised this woman, who had a gothic style, would like her pink dress. "Oh! Thank you."

King kept guiding her through the crowd, introducing her to Storm, Doc, Steele, Faust, and a handful of others. Most of them had women by their sides. Women who, Ella realized, all had a similar style as her. Soft fabrics, ruffles, bright colors. Cute rather than sexy.

She took in the scene around her, heart thumping as she noticed something else.

Off to the side, two women sat cross-legged on the pavement, completely engrossed in decorating the cement with pastel sidewalk chalk. Not far from them, another pair giggled as they climbed on a small playground structure, kicking their feet excitedly as they whooshed down the slide.

And then, a few yards away, one woman twirled in a fluffy tutu, blowing bubbles into the evening air.

Ella blinked, trying to make sense of it all. They were clearly adults.

Her mind whirled, trying to piece together what she was seeing. These women were playing, completely at ease, as if this were the most normal thing in the world.

A tiny thought wiggled into her mind, one she instantly dismissed as ridiculous.

Are they… Little?

She had read about it before. Littles, Caregivers, Daddy Doms. But that was fiction.

It wasn't real. Right?

You're being silly.

But she was Little, so why would it be silly for these other women to be as well?

As her eyes darted back to the couples she had met, she noticed another pattern. The way the men spoke to their women was soft but firm. The way the men's hands rested on the small of their women's backs, protective and steady. The way the women leaned into them, trusting, looking at them like they wanted them to lead.

Her gaze flicked to King, seeking reassurance. As if he could sense her uncertainty, he looked down at her and gave a small, gentle smile.

Soon, the scent of grilled meat filled the air, and King lifted his chin toward the serving table.

"Let's get you something to eat."

Ella followed, still processing everything. As they reached the food, King grabbed a plate and looked at her expectantly.

"What do you want?"

Ella blinked up at him. "Oh, um... I can get it."

King raised a brow. "I know you *can*. I'm asking what you *want*."

Her cheeks warmed as she hesitated. "Maybe... a burger?"

He chose a perfectly grilled patty and placed it on an open bun. "What else?"

"...Macaroni and cheese?"

A smirk. "Figured." He scooped a generous portion onto her plate. "Anything else?"

She chewed her lip, sneaking a glance at the juice boxes off to the side.

King followed her gaze, then, without pausing, grabbed one and set it on her plate.

Ella stared at him, heart doing something strange.

It wasn't just him.

Everywhere she looked, the other men were doing the same. Fixing plates, pouring drinks, and making sure their women had what they wanted. And not in an overbearing way, in a caring way.

She swallowed as she reached for her plate. "Thank you."

King's smirk softened. "Anytime, dollface."

Ella's breath hitched, but before she could overthink it, she thought she heard something. Just a whispered word from nearby.

A woman, leaning into her man, murmuring something so soft that Ella barely caught it.

"Thank you, Daddy."

Ella froze.

Had she misheard?

No. No way.

Her cheeks flamed as she quickly looked away, focusing on the food in her hands instead.

Her thoughts spun, trying to make sense of everything, but as she walked toward the tables with King, one question settled in her mind.

If the rest of the men here were Daddies, did that mean King was, too?

The warmth of the bonfire soothed Ella as she tucked her knees against her chest, watching the flames dance before her. The compound was quieter now, laughter and conversation mellowing as the evening stretched on. Most of the club members and their women were still chatting, some curled up in their men's laps, others wrapped in thick blankets.

She shivered slightly as a cool breeze whispered across her skin.

"Here."

Ella looked up as King draped a heavy blanket over her shoulders, his rough hands brushing against her arms for a second before he pulled away.

"Thank you," she said, pulling the soft fabric around herself.

King didn't respond, he just gave her a small nod before sitting beside her. They were slightly off to the side from the rest of the crowd, so it felt slightly intimate, but she didn't hate it one bit.

He stretched his legs out and leaned back in his chair, his expression relaxed as he stared into the fire.

After a moment, his deep voice broke their silence. "So... tell me about New York."

Ella blinked, caught off guard by the question. She glanced over at him, studying his sharp features.

"What do you want to know?" she asked softly.

King turned his head, his dark eyes steady. "Why did you leave? I mean, Shadowridge is a different world than New York. It must be a big change."

Ella inhaled slowly, hesitating. She wasn't sure how much to tell him about her life. Part of her felt like she shouldn't talk about how fortunate she'd been, but another part wanted to share everything with King.

Just be honest. Be yourself.

"I grew up in a world of... more," she finally explained. "More money, more expectations, more pressure to be someone I never really felt I was." She looked down, picking at the blanket. "My parents are the type who care about appearances. Who you know, where you went to school, how much money you made. I always felt like I was playing a part, and I hated it."

King didn't interrupt. He just listened.

Ella exhaled. "I always wanted something simpler. A town where people actually know each other and treat each other with kindness and help each other when needed. Where life isn't about how much is in your bank account. My parents were born and bred to take after their parents in that respect, but they've always encouraged me to live how I want to, so they didn't put up too much of a fuss about me moving away. Anyway, I guess that's why I chose Shadowridge."

She glanced up at him, expecting some sort of judgment—maybe even amusement. But there was none. If anything, she almost thought she saw pride in his gaze.

"That why you took the job with the mayor?" King asked.

She shrugged. "It felt like the best way to actually belong here. To be part of the community and give something back."

King gave a small hum of approval, and the sound made a warmth settle in her chest.

For the first time in as long as Ella could remember, she felt like someone saw her.

"What about *your* parents?" She tilted her head toward him.

King leaned back, resting an arm over his knee. "Still in town. Been together since they were teenagers. They're great people. I don't talk to them as much as I'd like because my schedule is hectic but when we talk and see each other, we're close."

Ella smiled softly. "That's really nice."

He nodded. "They're good people. Always supported me, even when I was a little shit growing up."

She giggled. "I can't picture you being a little shit."

King smirked, shooting her a sideways glance. "That's because you didn't know me back then."

Ella shook her head, smiling to herself.

But before she could respond, a soft voice nearby caught her attention.

"Thank you, Daddy."

Her breath hitched.

Ella's gaze flicked toward the group, her stomach twisting as she realized what she'd heard.

It wasn't the first time tonight. She'd heard it earlier and thought maybe she was imagining things. But now... now, she was sure.

Her fingers tightened around the edge of the blanket.

King shifted beside her. "Something on your mind, princess?"

Ella swallowed, glancing up at him. His expression was unreadable, but there was something knowing in the way he looked at her, something that made her cheeks burn.

Finally, she forced herself to speak, her voice barely above a whisper. "Why do they... call them that?"

King didn't answer right away. Instead, he let the question hang in the air, watching her closely. Then, slowly, he smiled.

"I'm pretty sure you already know the answer to that, dollface."

Ella's entire face flamed.

She looked away quickly, her heart racing.

Oh my God.

King chuckled, low and deep, but he didn't say anything. He let her sit with it, let her process.

For a long while, they sat in comfortable silence, the fire crackling in front of them. Ella hadn't realized how tired she was until her body started sinking into the warmth of the blanket.

She must have drifted because the next thing she knew, King's deep voice was calling her name.

"Ella."

She blinked, lifting her head slightly. Only a few people remained outside, most of them men standing by the fire while sharing beers.

King was watching her, his smirk now replaced with something softer. "You're half asleep. You can crash at my place. I'll take the couch."

Ella straightened slightly, shaking her head. "No, no, I'm fine. I can drive."

King didn't look convinced. He sighed, then reached into his pocket, pulling out his phone.

"Fine. But take my number." He handed her his phone, watching as she typed in her number before sending herself a message. When she handed it back, he met her eyes, serious now. "Text me the moment you get home. Don't make me come and look for you because I won't be happy about it when I do."

Ella's stomach flipped.

She nodded, tucking her phone away. "I will."

King exhaled, clearly not thrilled but letting it go.

As they reached her car, a quiet awkwardness settled between them, heavy in the cool night air.

Ella turned to him, unsure what to say. "I had a really nice time tonight."

King didn't reply right away. He stared at her for a long moment, something unreadable in his eyes.

Then, before she could react, he reached out, his large hand curling gently around the back of her neck.

Ella inhaled sharply, her pulse hammering as he pulled her in —not for a kiss, but a hug.

A solid, warm, grounding hug.

His scent wrapped around her, smoky and masculine, and she melted into it, gripping the front of his shirt without thinking.

He held her for a second longer than necessary before pulling back, his thumb brushing against the side of her neck before dropping away completely.

"Drive safe, dollface."

Ella barely managed a nod before sliding into her car, her hands shaking as she held the steering wheel.

As she pulled out of the lot, her mind raced with everything that had happened. The people, the atmosphere, the *Daddy* comments...

But most of all, she couldn't stop thinking about how King had held her.

And the way she hadn't wanted to let go.

SIX
KING

King sat at the clubhouse bar, one hand wrapped around a cold beer, the other resting on his phone. The screen was dark, but that didn't stop him from staring at it, his fingers tapping absently against the worn wooden counter.

It had been four days.

Four days since the BBQ. Since he watched Ella drive away, gripping the wheel like she was afraid of whatever the hell was developing between them. Since she'd pressed herself into his chest during that hug, soft and warm, making it so damn hard to let go.

They hadn't texted. Not other than her sending a message to say that she'd gotten home safely and him saying goodnight.

He'd been waiting. For what, he wasn't sure. Maybe for her to reach out first. Maybe to see if his growing feelings for her would disappear because he barely knew the woman. He couldn't possibly have such strong emotions for her already. It was a simple infatuation. Surely if he fucked her, those feelings would disappear like they always did with other women. But Ella was Little. Undeniably Little, and the last thing he wanted to do was hurt her or lead her on.

He picked up his phone again, thumb hovering over her name in his contacts. He could text her. It wasn't a big deal. A simple, *hey, how's it going?* would do. Or maybe something playful—*did you survive off candy salad for the last four days, or did you cave and eat real food?*

Fucking candy salad. Only Ella would think of something like that. Brightly colored and sugary. Just like her.

But every time he thought about hitting send, he hesitated.

And he *never* hesitated. It wasn't his style.

A low chuckle sounded beside him. "Jesus, man. Just text her already."

King turned his head, finding Gabriel dropping onto the barstool next to him, a beer in his hand, eyes glittering with amusement.

King grunted. "Didn't say I was going to text her."

Gabriel snorted. "Didn't have to. You've been staring at your phone for days."

King rolled his shoulders, taking a slow sip of his beer. Outside, a bunch of the Littles were playing in the yard. Giggling and chasing each other, completely lost in their own world. It was adorable, and he could picture Ella playing with them.

King found himself drawn to them, watching as Harper and Ivy knelt on the pavement, lost in another round of sidewalk chalk, while a couple of others squealed as they tumbled down the playground slide. It was peaceful here, familiar. But it wasn't settling the tension winding through him because all he wanted was for Ella to be out there, too.

Gabriel followed his gaze, his smirk softening. "Why are you being so stubborn? You can have what we all have. I saw the way she looked at you."

King arched a brow. "What?"

Gabriel glanced toward the Littles. "She looked at you like Eden looks at me. Like Ivy looks at Steele."

King didn't respond right away, just exhaled slowly through his nose. He'd thought that, too, but hadn't wanted to assume.

Gabriel huffed out a quiet laugh, shaking his head. "Text her. She's waiting for you to take the lead. Little girls often struggle with making decisions. You know that. She probably wants to text you, but she's second-guessing it. So quit being a wimp and take charge. Send that text."

King clenched his jaw, taking another pull from his beer.

He wasn't wrong.

There was something about Ella. Something he couldn't shake, couldn't get out of his damn head. She was soft but not fragile, sweet but not naïve. She was playful in a way she didn't even realize, and the way she had reacted to the club's women at the BBQ? He had no doubt about her being Little. Which meant he needed to take the lead.

Gabriel leaned back, smirking. "Good luck. I'm gonna go push my girl on the swing before she has a full-blown tantrum that turns into her getting her bottom spanked."

King laughed because as he looked out at the playground, it looked like Eden was already in the middle of a tantrum as she scowled at Gabriel and kicked her feet wildly trying to get the swing to move on its own.

With a long breath, he looked at his phone again.

And this time, he didn't overthink it.

> King: You eat any real food this week, dollface? Or you still surviving on candy salad?

As soon as he sent it, it was like he could finally breathe.

King barely had time to set his beer down before his phone buzzed in his hand. He smiled, already knowing it was her before even looking at the screen.

> Ella: Excuse you, candy salad is a very sophisticated dish.

King huffed out a laugh, shaking his head.

> King: Yeah? What's the main course? Gummy bear stew?

There was a short pause before his phone buzzed again.

> Ella: Don't be ridiculous. Gummy bears are for dessert. The main course was a balanced meal of Goldfish crackers and a juice box.

King let out a low chuckle, running a hand over his jaw. *Christ, this woman.*

> King: And here I was, worried about your diet. Sounds like you're thriving.

> Ella: Oh, I am. Top-tier nutrition over here.

> King: Guess I can stop losing sleep over it, then.

> Ella: Wait... you've been losing sleep over me?

King paused for half a second. He could practically *see* the playful challenge in her words, the teasing tilt of her head as she waited for his response.

> King: Maybe a little. Just don't wanna be responsible for you passing out from a sugar crash.

A long pause. Then—

> Ella: I've only passed out from a sugar crash once today.

King huffed out a laugh, shaking his head.

She was trouble. And he really was worried about her nutrition. Especially after learning about her life in New York. It was possible she'd never cooked a real meal before.

> King: You working tomorrow?

Ella: Yep! Gotta make copies, file things, be an all-around office rockstar. Why?

> King: Because I'll be coming in for my shift tomorrow morning, and I expect you to have eaten an actual meal before I get there.

Ella: Bold of you to assume I take orders from you.

> King: You don't.

Ella: Good.

> King: Yet.

Ella didn't reply right away. King smirked, knowing that message had probably got her flustered. He could practically feel her overthinking her response.

A minute later, his phone buzzed again.

Ella: ...Rude.

King chuckled, settling back against the bar.

> King: Sleep well, dollface. Looking forward to seeing you tomorrow. Try not to dream of me too much.

This time, her response was instant.

Ella: Ha! You wish. Night, King.

King grinned.
Damn right, he did.

King stepped into the firehouse, his bag slung over one shoulder. His shift was about to start, but before he got to work, he had one stop to make.

Ella's office.

She was already at her desk, typing away on her laptop. Her hair was pulled up in another high ponytail, and today's outfit was just as soft and colorful as ever. An oversized pastel sweater and a skirt that barely brushed her knees.

She looked up when he approached, her lips parting slightly in surprise. "King!"

He grinned, setting a black plastic container down on her desk.

"What's this?" she asked, eyeing it with curiousity.

"A true balanced lunch for *Little* girls."

Ella's entire body went still.

Her lips parted, but no words came out. A deep flush crept up her neck, her hands tightening on the armrests of her chair. She blinked at him, wide-eyed, caught somewhere between shock and something else. Arousal? Curiosity? He wasn't sure.

King held her gaze. He wasn't going to push her. Not yet.

After a long moment, she finally managed to find her voice. "...King."

"Mhm?"

She narrowed her eyes slightly, a mixture of suspicion and interest. "...What's in the container?"

He leaned down, bracing his hands on the desk, dropping his voice low enough for only her to hear.

"Chicken, rice, vegetables." He paused before continuing, "And fruit snacks along with a juice box."

Ella sucked in a sharp breath.

King grinned, straightening. "Eat it, dollface."

She exhaled shakily, glaring at him even though her face was pink. "You're bossy."

"Yep," he agreed easily.

Ella rolled her eyes, shaking her head. But there was no real heat behind it, only something warm and flustered.

King let the silence hang for a beat before he leaned in again, his voice quieter this time. "Let me take you out after the end of my shift on Friday."

Ella's breath caught.

"A date," he clarified, in case there was any doubt.

She stared at him for a long moment, then finally nodded, a small smile tugging at her lips. "Okay."

"Good."

"Thank you for lunch."

King winked at her. "You're welcome. Be good, Little one."

Her blush deepened at the nickname, but she didn't argue. When he glanced back at her, he was more than pleased to find her watching him as he walked away.

Over the next few days, while he was on shift, King and Ella spent nearly all their free time texting. The conversations were easy, full of teasing and playful banter, but every so often, they dipped into something a little deeper.

> King: You ever gonna admit that I make better meals than you?

> Ella: Never. I stand by my candy salad love.

> King: That's why you let me feed you real food, huh?

> Ella: I let you because it makes you happy.

King smirked at that, leaning back on the firehouse couch, his thumb hovering over the screen before he typed his next message. It did make him happy that she ate the food he left on her desk whenever she was there.

> King: So what makes you happy, dollface?

A pause. Then—

> Ella: Lots of things.

> King: Like? I want to know you, Little one.

Another pause.

> Ella: Coloring. Soft blankets. Bubble baths. Stuffies. Movies.

King's chest tightened slightly.

> King: That so?

> Ella: ...Yes?

He could almost hear the uncertainty in her response, the nervous energy behind it.

He decided to push—just a bit.

> King: What else do you like to do when you're in Little Space?

This time, the pause was longer. King waited, watching the screen, knowing she was debating how much to say.

When her response finally came, it was hesitant but honest.

Ella: I don't really... I mean, I never really called it that before. I don't know if I really have Little Space.

King: You do.

Ella: ...How do you know?

King: Because I see you, dollface.

No response.

King didn't push.

A few minutes later, his phone finally buzzed again.

Ella: I like to color. And build puzzles. And drink from cute cups with those spouts. And I like soft things. And sometimes, I just like to be small.

King exhaled slowly, something settling deep in his chest.

King: That's good, baby. You should get to feel small whenever you need to.

Another long pause.

Ella: Baby?

King: Yeah.

Ella: ...I don't hate it.

King: Good.

SEVEN

ELLA

Ella sat on the floor of the firehouse storage room, surrounded by boxes of canned goods and non-perishable items, carefully sorting through the donations for the upcoming food drive. She had already organized most of the items into neat stacks, but there was still a long way to go.

Not that she minded.

She liked it here. She liked that she was doing something that mattered. Something that would make a difference. Make the world a better place.

She wiped her forehead with the back of her hand, sighing as she reached for another can of green beans. Maybe she should take a break soon. She'd been working all morning. Mostly because she was trying to keep her mind busy so she didn't think too hard about the date she was going on with King on Friday. Because if she thought about it too hard, she would overthink it, and she didn't want to do that. She liked King. A lot. Which was both exciting and terrifying.

Before she had time for a break, a familiar shadow appeared over her.

"Drink your water."

Ella blinked, looking up.

King stood in the doorway, arms crossed, watching her like a man who knew he was in charge, even though she hadn't exactly agreed to that. Yet.

She arched a brow, tilting her head. "Excuse me?"

King pointed to the unopened bottle of water sitting on the table beside her. "Water. Drink it."

Ella scoffed, picking up another can to stack instead. "You're not the boss of me."

The second the words left her mouth, she realized her mistake.

King's smirk was instant, slow and dangerous, his dark eyes flashing with something downright wicked.

"Dollface," he drawled, stepping forward, crouching in front of her so they were almost at eye-level. "You keep challenging me like that and I'm gonna have to do something about it."

Ella's breath hitched.

Heat crept up her neck, her fingers tightening around the can in her hands. She knew he was teasing her, but that look, the one that said he was *very* aware of how flustered she was, made her stomach flip in a way she didn't know how to handle.

So, naturally, she went on the defense.

She lifted her chin. "Oh yeah? Like what?"

King didn't break eye contact. Didn't blink.

And then, ever so casually, he reached over, grabbed the water bottle, unscrewed the cap, and held it out to her.

"Drink," he said, voice deep and certain. "Now."

Ella narrowed her eyes. "You would make a terrible waiter."

King huffed out a low chuckle, shaking his head. "Little girl, you're really testing me today."

She grinned, grabbing the bottle, but not before muttering, "Bossy."

King heard it.

She knew he had.

Because as she took a sip, just enough to appease him, he

leaned in slightly, voice dropping so low it sent a shiver down her spine.

"You don't even know what bossy looks like yet. But you will."

Ella choked.

On water.

King laughed outright, standing up as she sputtered, her face heating to an embarrassing degree.

"Careful now," he teased, patting the top of her head like she was helpless. "Wouldn't want you passing out before you finish sorting all this."

Ella scowled at him, glaring up from where she still sat on the floor. "I don't think I like you very much."

King grinned, reaching for the door. "Sure you do, baby."

Ella threw a can of corn at him as he walked away.

And the cocky man caught it without even turning around and chuckled.

Crap. She was in way over her head.

Later that day, she was lost in her work when a familiar deep voice interrupted her thoughts.

"Dollface."

She looked up, her heart giving its usual flutter as King leaned against the doorframe of her tiny office. His presence was always effortlessly commanding, like he belonged in every room he walked into.

"Hi," she replied. "What's up?"

"Remi texted me."

Ella blinked. "Remi?"

Remi was the goth Little at the BBQ. Even though the woman had been dressed head to toe in black, she was just like all the other Littles. Bubbly, playful, and friendly. All the girls had been. Ella had stuck close to King the entire night, but whenever they were near her, they'd included her in their conversations and had even mentioned their book club to her.

King nodded. "She wants your number."

Ella's breath caught.

Remi wants my number?

Her stomach flipped. In New York, Ella had known other women, but she'd never called them friends. Women in her family's social circles were never more than acquaintances. People they were supposed to rub elbows with at fancy events. It had been lonely living like that.

She was pretty sure Remi and the other women were the total opposite of the people she'd known back home. They thrived on real connections, and Ella wanted to be part of that. Was that why Remi wanted her number? Maybe?

"Oh." She shifted in her seat, suddenly feeling shy. "She—she does?"

King arched a brow as he looked at her curiously. "Is… that a problem? I can tell her no."

"No! I mean—" She cleared her throat, trying to play it cool. "You can give it to her."

King chuckled, shaking his head as he pushed off the doorframe. "Okay, dollface. Don't forget to drink your water."

And just like that, he was gone, leaving Ella staring at his muscular backside. She bet she could bounce a quarter off his firm ass. The thought made her giggle out loud as she turned back to her laptop.

A few minutes later, her screen lit up with a new message.

Remi: Hi! This is Remi—King gave me your number. Would you want to come over tonight? We're having our book club at the clubhouse.

Ella grinned, her excitement bubbling over as she quickly typed back.

Ella: I'd love to! What time?

Remi responded immediately, sending over details. Ella couldn't stop smiling. She had *plans*. With *friends*.

She had to tell King.

Still clutching her phone, she got up from her chair and made her way toward the bay. She had a feeling he was going to be thrilled for her. King had told her at the BBQ that the girls would want to befriend her, but she hadn't truly believed him. Until now. She could already picture the smug look on his handsome face when she told him.

But the second she stepped into the open space, she stopped short.

Her breath caught in her throat.

A woman stood in front of King. Close. *Too* close. She was tall, curvy, gorgeous, with long dark hair and a sexy smile. She tilted her head slightly, batting her eyelashes as she spoke to him, her expression flirtatious and warm.

Ella's stomach twisted.

They were too far away for her to hear the conversation, but she didn't need to. She saw it. The way the woman reached out, letting her fingers trail down King's arm. The way she laughed, shifting her weight so her body leaned in just enough to be noticeable.

Ella swallowed, something hot and ugly curling in her chest.

King didn't push her away. He stood there, staring at her, completely focused on whatever she was saying.

Ella's fingers tightened around her phone.

She had no right to feel this way.

King wasn't hers. They weren't together.

But for the first time since she'd met him, she felt stupid. Stupid for thinking there was something special about how he treated her. Stupid for believing she might be the only one getting his attention. One date didn't mean they were exclusive.

Her throat felt like it was closing in.

Slowly, she took a step back.

Then another.

Before she could even think about it, she grabbed her bag and laptop from her office, then slipped outside through another door, making her way to her car as quickly and quietly as possible.

She needed to get out of there before she started crying. She didn't want anyone to see her cry. Especially not King.

By the time she pulled away from the firehouse, her cheeks were wet and her excitement about book club had dimmed, leaving only a hollow ache in its place.

EIGHT
KING

King wiped down the side of the truck, his muscles working through the familiar motion as his mind drifted to a certain someone.

Little Ella.

His phone vibrated on the nearby workbench, and he grabbed it with one hand, smiling when he saw the latest text from Remi.

> Remi: She said yes! Ella's coming to book club tonight!

Another buzz.

> Remi: Told you she's one of us. She just doesn't know it yet.

King exhaled through his nose, shaking his head. He *did* know it. The moment he saw Ella at the BBQ, taking in all the Littles while they did the same, he knew they would be pulling her into their friendship circle. He couldn't be happier for her. When Ella had told him about her life in New York, he'd gotten the feeling that she'd been lonely there, so this would be really special for her.

He had just tucked his phone away when movement in his peripheral caught his attention.

He barely had time to react before a pair of soft, manicured hands wrapped around his waist from behind, pressing a feminine body against his back.

King stiffened instantly.

"Hey, baby," a sultry voice purred.

Fuck.

He turned his head slightly, jaw already tightening. "Janelle."

She stepped around him, pressing herself close. Too close. Her long dark hair was curled to perfection, her lips painted red, and the dress she wore, if it could even be called that, was tight, short, and low-cut.

The kind of thing that had once turned his head.

Not anymore.

"I was hoping I'd find you here," she said, dragging a single painted nail down his arm. "It's been too long, Daddy."

King gritted his teeth, stepping back, putting space between them. That word off her tongue made him want to vomit. "What do you want, Janelle?"

She pouted, ignoring his tone. "You. Obviously."

King exhaled sharply. "Not happening."

Janelle smiled like she didn't believe him. "Come on, baby. Don't be like that. I miss you."

King barely heard her.

Because *everything* about this moment was wrong.

His mind wasn't here. It wasn't on Janelle or whatever game she thought she was playing. It was still on his damn phone, reading the text Remi had sent him.

It was on Ella.

Ella, who had blushed when he'd brought her food earlier. Ella, who had looked so damn excited when he told her Remi wanted her number. Ella, who had no clue how much he was already thinking about her.

And that was the difference.

With Ella, he *wanted* to take care of her.

With Janelle, it had always been about something else. Something superficial. Temporary.

Something that wasn't at all real.

Janelle stepped closer again, her fingers trailing up his chest. "Come on, Daddy," she whispered. "We were good together. I miss you."

"No, we weren't," he snapped.

She ignored him, biting her lip in a way that once would've worked on him. Now, he recognized it as a fake move to get him to react. "Just one more chance. Let me remind you of how good it was."

He stared at her blankly, her words not even reaching him. The more she spoke, the more he zoned out, his expression flat as he let her spew more lies and bullshit to him.

Then, when she finally stopped talking, she reached for him, hands sliding toward his neck as she leaned in for a kiss.

King immediately took a step back, his expression hard. "Janelle." His voice was low and hard. "Leave."

For a second, her face twisted. Janelle wasn't used to being rejected. Then, with a sharp huff, she spun on her heel and stormed off, her heels clicking against the concrete.

King didn't watch her go.

Didn't care.

Because the second she disappeared, his mind snapped back to where it wanted to be.

Ella.

He wanted to be near her. To feel her sweetness surrounding him. Because she was real, and she was who he wanted. More than he'd realized.

He turned on his heel, striding inside, already moving toward her office.

But when he got there, it was empty.

King sat on the bench outside the firehouse, elbows resting on his knees, phone in hand. The screen glowed in the darkness, the last message he'd sent still sitting there.

Delivered.

But not read.

It had been hours.

His thumb hovered over the screen before he tapped out another.

> King: Hey, you okay?

He waited.

Nothing.

Frowning, he leaned against the cool brick wall behind him, staring at the night sky. It had been hours since he last saw Ella, hours since she had disappeared from the firehouse without a word.

And now she wasn't answering him.

His chest tightened.

He tried again.

> King: Ella?

A minute passed. Two. Three.

Still nothing.

He growled a curse under his breath, rubbing a hand over his jaw. He may not have known her for that long, but he knew Ella wasn't the type to ignore people, not unless something was wrong.

And he had a damn good guess as to what that *something* was.

Janelle.

She must have seen her. Seen the way she was all over him.

Even though he had shut that shit down fast. What if Ella thought there was more to it? What if she thought he *wanted* Janelle?

His stomach clenched.

No. That was the *last thing* he wanted.

Ella had to know that.

Didn't she?

He thought he'd made it pretty fucking clear. But maybe not clear enough.

He exhaled sharply, finding another contact.

> King: Remi, did Ella show up to book club?

The response came fast.

> Remi: Yeah, she's here.

King sagged with relief. At least she was safe. Being a firefighter made him think the worst-case scenario. And he'd be having that conversation with her about not responding once he figured out how to fix whatever was wrong. She might not be his yet, but he needed her to know that even if she was upset with him, he needed a response confirming she was okay. Before he could type anything else to Remi, another message popped up.

> Remi: She's quiet. Something's wrong. She won't say what.

Damn it.

His grip on the phone tightened.

> King: Tell her to call me. Or text me. Just… tell her to talk to me.

Remi sent a thumbs-up emoji, but King wasn't sure if it meant she'd actually listen. Those Littles stuck together like glue.

Hours passed.

The firehouse stayed busy. Checking equipment, going over drills, a couple of minor calls. But through it all, King kept checking his phone, waiting for a buzz, a notification. *Something.*

Nothing came.

By the time he was in his bunk, staring at the ceiling, his gut was twisted in knots.

Ella had seen Janelle. He knew it. It was one more reason he couldn't stand that woman.

Because now, Ella was shutting him out.

He might've managed to ruin this before it even started.

NINE
ELLA

E lla wrapped her arms around herself as she stepped inside the clubhouse, her excitement for book club buried under a heavy weight in her chest. The other girls were already curled up on chairs and bean bags in a small nook of a room off the common area, chatting animatedly, clutching their books and drinks.

She'd only come tonight because she knew King wouldn't be here. She didn't think she could handle seeing him right now, not after what she'd witnessed earlier at the firehouse. Not only was she sad, she was embarrassed, too.

Ella took a seat on the couch next to Remi, pulling her knees up to her chest.

Remi's eyes flicked over her, immediately laced with concern. "What's wrong?" she asked quietly, leaning in.

Ella forced a smile. "Just tired."

Remi didn't look convinced, though she didn't push. Instead, she passed Ella a copy of the book they were reading, and the discussion started.

Ella tried to listen, but the words blurred together. Her mind kept replaying the image of that woman, the way she'd touched King, the way she'd looked at him. Like she belonged with him.

Like she belonged by his side. It was obvious they knew each other well. And why would he pick Ella over someone sexy and sophisticated like that? With perky cleavage and glowing skin. Ella couldn't compete, even on her best day. Her breasts certainly had never looked that good, no matter what kind of bra she'd tried.

She'd barely noticed when Remi's phone buzzed beside her. A few minutes later, Remi cleared her throat.

"So," she said casually, though her tone was anything but, "what did King do?"

She snapped her head up. "What?"

The room quieted.

The other girls turned to look at her, curiosity in their eyes.

Remi tilted her head, lips twitching like she was holding back a smirk. "Do we need to go kick his butt? Because we will."

"Oh, heck yeah," Ivy added. "We can put slime on the seat of his bike."

Crap. She didn't want them to do that.

Ella's cheeks burned. "No, he didn't—" She hesitated, chewing on her lip. "It's stupid."

"Doubt it," Harper said, crossing her arms. "Spill."

Ella exhaled, feeling ridiculous even saying it aloud. "There was a woman at the firehouse today," she admitted. "She was gorgeous. And sophisticated. Way more King's type than me. And she was all over him."

Carlee frowned. "Did he touch her back?"

Ella hesitated. "I don't know. I left before I could see."

Harper pulled out her phone, typing something quickly. A moment later, she sighed dramatically. "My Daddy says she's King's *ex*. She's called Janelle." She looked up. "And he hates her."

It took Ella a moment to remember that Doc was Harper's Daddy. She'd seen him several times at the firehouse. He was one of the medics there.

"He does?" Ella asked.

Harper bobbed her head. "Apparently, they broke up forever ago. She cheated. He won't even give her the time of day."

Ella shifted uncomfortably, doubt still making her stomach twist. "It... it didn't look like that."

Remi rolled her eyes. "Trust me, if King were interested in her, we'd all know it. That man doesn't hide what he wants. And it was obvious at the BBQ that he wants you."

Ella wanted to believe them.

But the image of that woman pressing herself against King was burned into her mind.

And no matter what they said, the doubt wouldn't go away.

Ella stepped into her tiny house, the quiet bothering her more than it had since she'd moved from New York. Normally, coming home felt comforting. Her own little space full of warmth, softness, and things that made her feel safe. But tonight, everything felt off.

She moved through the motions of getting ready for bed, trying to shake off the lingering sadness. After slipping into her favorite pair of footie pajamas, light pink with miniscule white clouds, she let out a small sigh. She hugged her stuffed bunny to her chest, running her fingers over its soft fur as she climbed into bed.

Her phone sat on the nightstand, the screen glowing with unread messages.

From him.

Ella swallowed hard, her fingers trembling slightly as she picked it up.

She hadn't checked them since she left the firehouse. She knew she should've opened them sooner, but she was afraid. Afraid of what he might say. Afraid that he wouldn't even bother explaining. Afraid that he would, and it wouldn't be one she wanted.

Taking a deep breath, she tapped the screen and began reading.

> King: Ella?
>
> King: Did I do something?
>
> King: Talk to me, Little one.
>
> King: Please.
>
> King: Remi says you're at book club, so I know you're okay. But I need to know if you're upset with me.
>
> King: If you saw something today, let me explain. Just... don't shut me out.

Her chest tightened.

He knew.

Of course, he did.

King wasn't stupid. He had probably put the pieces together the second she left. But even though his messages sounded sincere, she still couldn't bring herself to reply.

Not yet.

Instead, she set her phone back on the nightstand, turning onto her side and curling into a small ball, clutching her bunny close.

She tried to tell herself it didn't matter. That she shouldn't be *this* upset over a man she barely knew.

But it did matter because she had developed feelings for King in the short time they'd known each other.

And now her heart hurt more than she'd ever expected.

Ella kept her focus on her computer screen, fingers typing aimlessly as she tried to push past the strange, unsettled feeling lingering from the night before. She had struggled to sleep, her mind replaying the image of King and that woman over and over again. Even after the girls at book club had insisted there was nothing to worry about, doubt still gnawed at her.

A knock on her office door made her glance up. Before she could respond, the door opened, and her breath caught as she rose from her seat.

King.

Dressed in his firehouse uniform, he filled the small space effortlessly, his broad frame making the office seem even smaller than it already was, which was basically a closet. His expression was unreadable, but his sharp eyes were locked on her with determination.

"Morning, Ella," he greeted, his voice low and steady.

She forced a smile. "Morning."

He studied her for a moment, then stepped inside and shut the door behind him. The click of the latch sent a ripple of tension through her.

"King—"

"Sit," he instructed, motioning to her chair before sinking into the one across from her.

Ella hesitated. She wanted to brush past this, to pretend it hadn't affected her, but King wasn't going to let that happen.

So, she did as she was told.

He leaned forward, resting his forearms on his knees. "I know why you left yesterday."

She swallowed hard, keeping her expression neutral. "I don't know what you mean."

He exhaled sharply, shaking his head. "Don't do that, Little one. Don't lie. I won't lie to you, and I expect the same respect *from* you. You saw my ex at the firehouse, and you assumed something that wasn't true."

Her stomach tightened. "I didn't assume anything."

He arched a brow. "Really? Then why'd you leave without a word? Why'd you ignore my texts?"

Ella's gaze flickered to the side, shame creeping in. "I was just tired."

"That's three, dollface. Three times you've lied to me. If you were mine, which one day you will be, you'd have a very sore bottom for doing something like that," he said sternly.

She shifted in her chair, hugging her arms to her chest while trying to ignore her throbbing clit. "It's no big deal, King. What you do or who you see isn't my business."

"It *is* a big deal," he countered. "Listen to me, baby. That woman? She means *nothing* to me. I didn't even know she was going to show up. We haven't spoken in over a year, and I have no desire to start now."

Ella glanced up at him hesitantly. "Why'd she come back?"

King's jaw ticked. "Hell, if I know. She tried to pull the whole *I miss you, I made a mistake* routine, but I shut her down immediately. The only reason I listened to her at all was because I didn't want to cause a scene at work. I didn't touch her or return any of her advances. I told her to leave."

"Oh."

His eyes softened. "The only person I want, Ella, the only one I see, is you."

Her lips parted slightly as his words sank in. He looked so sincere, his expression open and raw. The doubt that had clouded her mind began to clear.

"You really mean that?" she asked, barely above a whisper.

King nodded, his gaze unwavering. "Yeah, baby girl. I really mean that."

Ella breathed out slowly, letting the tension in her shoulders ease. He wasn't lying. She could feel it, see it in the way he looked at her.

"Okay," she murmured.

His face relaxed, and he let out a deep breath, too, as though he was relieved. "Does that mean you'll still go out with me tonight?"

A small smile tugged at the corner of her mouth. "Yeah. I'd like that."

King grinned, wide and perfect. "Good."

He stood then, making his way around her desk. Ella's pulse spiked as he leaned down, bracing his hands on either arm of her chair, effectively caging her in.

"The only person I think about is you," he whispered, his words warm against her temple. "And if I'm lucky enough, maybe one day I'll earn the title of your Daddy."

Ella's breath caught, her entire body tingling at what he'd said. Before she could respond, he pressed a lingering kiss to the top of her head, his fresh scent surrounding her.

Then he pulled back, a smug smile on his lips as though he knew exactly the effect he was having on her. "I'll pick you up at seven, dollface. Text me your address."

With that, he was gone, leaving Ella sitting at her desk, her heart pounding, her cheeks burning, and her core aching with need.

TEN

KING

King inhaled deeply as he stepped up to Ella's front door, rolling his shoulders in an attempt to shake off the unfamiliar nervous energy coursing through him. He knocked twice, and within moments, the door cracked open, revealing Ella wearing a soft, flowy dress that made her look even smaller than she already was. Her hair was down, curls tumbling around her shoulders, and she fidgeted with the hem of her dress, her big eyes flicking up to meet his. She looked adorable.

"Hey, Little one," he murmured, a slow smile tugging at his lips.

"Hi," she replied softly, shifting on her feet.

King leaned against the doorframe, his gaze flicking over the tiny but cozy space behind her. "I like your home. It suits you."

Ella's cheeks pinkened, and she tucked a strand of hair behind her ear. "Thanks. It's still a work in progress."

"Well, from what I can see, it's perfect."

She ducked her head, and he swore she was trying not to smile too big. He liked that. Liked knowing he could make her shy with just a few words.

"You ready to go?" he asked.

She smiled, grabbing her small purse before stepping outside. He guided her toward his truck with a hand at the small of her back, opening the passenger door for her. Once she was settled inside and he'd reached over her to buckle her in, he climbed into the driver's seat and started the engine.

"Where are we going?" she asked as they pulled out of her driveway.

"You'll see."

She narrowed her eyes at him. "If you take me somewhere weird, I'm calling the cops."

He barked out a laugh. "You're a menace."

"I'm just saying. I watch *a lot* of true crime," she said, crossing her arms.

"Noted and slightly concerned. Little girls shouldn't be watching shit like that. But don't worry, I'm taking you somewhere with *real* food. None of that candy salad nonsense."

Ella gasped, clutching her chest dramatically. "How dare you disrespect candy salad like that."

King shook his head, chuckling. "It's not food, Little one. It's sugar in a bowl."

"Psshhh, whatever. You just don't appreciate fine cuisine."

"You're lucky you're cute," he muttered, making her giggle.

When they arrived at the restaurant, he led her inside, escorting her toward a booth near the window. It was a laid-back, local steakhouse, not too fancy, but it served good food and was quiet enough that they could talk without shouting over the noise of other customers. As they sat, he wondered if it was too casual for her. She had told him she'd grown up wealthy, so this was probably a major step down from the expensive restaurants she was used to. Then he remembered that she left New York for a reason.

Once the menus were in front of them, King glanced at Ella. "You know what you want, or do you want me to order for you?"

She bit her lip, then smiled softly. "You can order for me."

"Yeah?"

"I trust you."

Something warm settled in him at that. It was a big deal to him that she trusted him. Especially after the incident with Janelle. Even if it was just to order her dinner.

When the food arrived, he caught the way Ella's eyes lit up at the plate in front of her. A perfectly cooked steak, mashed potatoes, and roasted veggies. She wiggled a little in her seat, clearly excited.

King chuckled. "See? *Real* food."

Ella huffed. "Fine, I'll admit it looks good."

He grabbed his fork, speared a piece of steak, and held it out to her. "Want me to feed you?"

Her eyes went wide, and she let out a nervous giggle, shaking her head. "I—no, I can feed myself."

The want was there, but they were in a public space, so he understood her hesitance.

King leaned in slightly, his voice dropping. "Next time we're alone, I'm hand-feeding you."

Ella's breath hitched, and she pressed her thighs together, her blush deepening. She didn't argue, though.

Dinner was easy. Filled with laughter, teasing, and stories about their lives. King hadn't felt this light in years. Being with Ella was effortless, like she was meant to fit into his life. Nothing like how it had been with Janelle.

After dinner, he drove them to the drive-in theater outside of town.

Ella practically bounced in her seat when she saw where they were. "A drive-in? Oh my gosh, I've never been to one!"

King grinned. "Figured you'd like it."

He parked the truck with the bed facing the screen, then hopped out, grabbing a blanket and a few snacks from the back. When he pulled out a small baggie filled with colorful candy, Ella gasped.

"You *did not*—"

King held up the bag and winked. "Candy salad, just for you. For dessert."

She let out a delighted squeal and launched herself at him, throwing her arms around his neck. He caught her easily, laughing as she squeezed him tight.

"You're the best," she murmured against his shoulder.

He held her a second longer than necessary, then reluctantly let her go. "Yeah, yeah. Now get up in the truck bed before I change my mind."

When he lowered the tailgate, she gasped. He'd already put cushioned mats back there along with a bunch of throw pillows, and when he reached in and turned on the battery-operated fairy lights he lined around the edge of the bed, she turned her attention to him.

"King," she whispered. "This is... I can't believe you did all this for me. It's so beautiful I could cry."

His heart pounded against his ribcage as he watched her take it all in. It was something simple, yet it meant so much to her. He would do shit like this every day for Ella if it made her this happy.

"Let me help you up, dollface." Without waiting, he reached out and lifted her, then had to adjust his dick as he watched her crawl across the padding to get comfortable, flashing him a glimpse of her pink panties... which had lollipops printed on them. Of course.

They settled in, backs against the stack of pillows, a blanket draped over them as the old black-and-white movie flickered across the screen.

Ella sighed happily. "This is perfect."

King tightened his arm around her shoulders, pulling her into his side. "Yeah, baby. It is."

He wasn't talking about the movie, though. Not even close.

She snuggled into him, resting her head on his chest. His fingers absentmindedly traced up and down her arm, and he felt her slowly relax.

At one point, she shifted slightly, tilting her face toward his, and his breath caught. They were close—so close that all he had to do was lean down a fraction to kiss her.

Her gaze flicked to his lips, and he started to close the distance.

But just as he was about to kiss her, a loud crash from the movie made her jump slightly, breaking the moment.

King huffed a quiet laugh. "You okay, Little one?"

Her cheeks flushed as she giggled. "Yeah. Just got startled. Sheesh. What a way to ruin the moment."

He pulled her against him, rubbing slow circles on her back. "We'll have many more moments, dollface."

At least, he hoped they would. If he had it his way.

By the time the credits rolled, King glanced down and found Ella sound asleep against his chest, her tiny frame curled up under the blanket.

And her thumb was in her mouth. So innocent and sweet. He wondered if she had a pacifier at home. She needed one.

His heart clenched as he watched her.

Yeah, she was definitely his. She just didn't know it yet.

ELEVEN
ELLA

Ella stirred as she felt herself being lifted, the warmth surrounding her replaced by the cool night air. She blinked sluggishly, her head lolling against something solid and comforting.

King.

His strong arms held her close as he carried her from the back of his truck to the passenger seat.

"Mm," she mumbled sleepily, barely awake.

"Shh, Little one. Go back to sleep."

But as he set her in the seat, the loss of his warmth made her stir again. She forced her heavy eyelids open just as he reached across her, pulling the seatbelt over her body to buckle her in. His face hovered close. So close that she could see the flicker of the drive-in lights reflecting in his deep brown eyes.

She sucked in a breath, her pulse hammering in her neck.

He hesitated, his lips inches from hers, and for a second, she thought maybe she imagined the way his gaze flickered down to her mouth, the way his breath hitched.

Then, before she could think about it too much, he closed the distance.

The kiss was light, barely a brush of lips, but it sent a shiver down her spine. Her fingers curled in her lap, her legs pressing together as warmth pooled low in her belly.

King pulled back slowly, his lips twitching as he cupped her cheek for a brief moment.

"You're trouble," he murmured.

Ella swallowed hard, her face burning as she fidgeted.

The drive back to her house was quiet, tension filling the space between them. She kept sneaking glances, her mind replaying that soft kiss over and over. By the time they pulled into her driveway, her nerves were tangled in knots.

King put the truck in park and unbuckled his seatbelt, turning to her. "Come on, dollface. Let's get you inside."

She climbed out, her heart racing as he walked her to the house. She hesitated, fingers toying with her keys before she turned to look up at him.

"Do you, um…" She bit her lip, suddenly nervous. "Do you want to come in?"

King's eyes darkened slightly. "Yeah. I do."

She unlocked the door and stepped inside, flicking on a soft lamp in the living room. King followed her in, his presence overwhelming in the best way.

For a beat, they both stood there, unsure of what to do next.

Then King reached for Ella, his hands settling on her waist as he pulled her against him. His lips brushed over hers once—soft, teasing. But when she let out the smallest whimper, he groaned and deepened the kiss.

It started out slow and sweet, but within seconds, it turned into something more. Something demanding. His hands tightened on her, and she pressed onto her toes, her fingers gripping the front of his shirt. He kissed her like he was claiming her, like he'd been waiting for this moment as long as she had.

When he finally pulled back, they were both breathing hard.

His forehead rested against hers as he whispered, "You taste like candy, Little one."

She let out a shaky laugh, still dizzy from their kiss.

King lifted a hand, tracing his thumb over her flushed cheek. "Can I get you ready for bed, baby?"

Ella nodded automatically, then hesitated. "Yeah... but..." She swallowed. "No one's ever helped me before."

King's expression softened, and he brushed his fingers through her hair. "Then I guess it's time for a first... with me."

She stared up at him, her heart pounding.

"Starting with this," he murmured, tilting her chin up to press the softest kiss to her forehead.

And just like that, Ella knew she was a goner for this man.

Ella stood in the middle of her bedroom, her face warm as King moved toward her dresser. She felt like she was buzzing. Like her skin was extra sensitive after that kiss in the living room. She watched as he opened a drawer and sifted through her pajamas.

"This one's cute," he murmured, holding a soft pink nightie covered in tiny bunnies. His gaze flicked to her stuffed bunny on her bed. "Very fitting."

Ella covered her face with her hands, groaning. "You're embarrassing."

King chuckled, tossing the nightie onto the bed. "Go potty, Little one. Call me when you're done."

Her stomach flipped at the casual tone he said it in, like it was the most natural thing in the world. She bit her lip, nodding as she padded into the bathroom, shutting the door behind her. She sat on the toilet, trying to calm her racing heart. It was overwhelming—the way he took charge, the way he handled her with such care. But it was also amazing.

When she finished, she washed her hands and took a deep breath before opening the door.

King was waiting, leaning against the doorframe, arms crossed over his chest, that cocky grin tugging at his lips.

"Good girl," he praised.

Ella's face burned.

"Since your bathroom's so small, I'll let you brush your own teeth. But I'll be watching to make sure you do a good job. Especially after all that candy you ate at the drive-in."

Her jaw dropped. "You're *what?*"

"Go on, baby. Show me how well you brush those little teeth."

She huffed, her face impossibly warm as she grabbed her toothbrush and toothpaste. It was hard to focus with him leaning in the doorway, watching her like an overprotective Daddy. She tried to pretend he wasn't there, but that was pretty much impossible.

When she finally rinsed and set her toothbrush down, King held out his hand. "Wet washcloth."

Ella hesitated for half a second before grabbing one and running it under the faucet. She turned to hold it out to him. King wrapped his free hand around the back of her neck, gently tugging her closer.

Her breath hitched as he held her still with a gentle grip and brought the washcloth to her face. He wiped over her cheeks, her chin, the tip of her nose, slow and careful, looking after her like she was something precious.

Her stomach fluttered as he took care of her so easily. He was good at this.

"All clean," King murmured, brushing his thumb over her cheek before stepping back. "Good girl."

Ella swallowed, unsure if she could even form words at that moment.

He took her hand and led her back into the bedroom. She stood there, still dazed, as he glanced around, a soft smile tugging at his lips.

"I love your room," he said.

Ella shifted on her feet. "You do?"

"Yeah, baby. It's perfect for a Little girl."

Her heart squeezed.

Then his eyes flicked to the nightie on her bed. He pointed to it, his expression turning serious though there was still a little teasing in his eyes.

"I'm going to change your clothes," he told her, his voice steady. "If you don't want me to, you need to say red to stop me."

Ella's breath caught in her throat.

She knew what he was saying. He was giving her a way out, a safeword to use. But he was also telling her that if she didn't stop him, he was going to take care of her how he wanted to.

Ella's breath came in shallow pants as she stared up at King, her fingers twisting together in front of her. She knew she should say something, but all she could do was stand there, her entire body buzzing with nervous energy.

King held her gaze, giving her time, giving her space to stop him if she wanted. But she didn't.

His lips curved slightly. "Good girl. If you want me to stop at any time, say red. Nod or say yes if you understand."

Her knees nearly buckled as she nodded.

He stepped closer, and with slow, deliberate movements, he reached for the hem of her dress. His fingers brushed against her stomach as he pulled the fabric up, his knuckles warm against her skin. Ella lifted her arms instinctively, letting him slip the soft fabric over her head.

She shivered.

It wasn't like she'd never been undressed by a man before, but this wasn't the same. The only time she'd ever been intimate with someone had been sloppy and quick and so disappointing. With King, it was different. There was no rush, no expectation. Just him taking care of her, moving with ease like it was totally normal.

She gasped as he reached behind her, fingers skimming her back as he unhooked her bra.

The straps slid down her arms, and for a moment, she felt the flicker of embarrassment—felt herself teetering between her usual mindset and something softer, something deeper.

But King didn't leer, didn't gawk. He simply folded her bra neatly and set it with the rest of her clothes before reaching for her pajama nightie.

Ella stared at the soft, frilly fabric, her stomach flipping. It was one of her favorites.

"Arms up, baby."

Her hands trembled slightly as she lifted them, and when he slipped the nightie over her head, the fabric fell around her, brushing against her bare skin like a whisper.

She swallowed hard, her nipples pebbled and aching. He'd seen her breasts and had acted like a gentleman. Like a Daddy.

Ella's breath came out in a shudder.

King's presence, his touch, his voice—it was all so careful, so steady. She felt small, the tension in her body melting away while standing in her nightie and panties in front of him

And that's when it happened.

That familiar, floaty feeling settled over her, warm and consuming. Her limbs felt lighter, her thoughts quieter. The grown-up worries, the insecurities, the doubts—they all started to fade, replaced by something soft and safe.

She blinked up at King, her fingers curling into the hem of her nightie as she swayed slightly on her feet.

"You okay, Little one?" he asked, his voice a hushed murmur. "Think I need to get you a lovey to hold in your hand when you feel fidgety."

Ella nodded slowly, feeling small, feeling so incredibly Little.

King reached out, running his fingers gently through her hair before cupping her cheek. His thumb brushed her skin, grounding her, anchoring her.

"Yeah," he murmured, tilting his head as he studied her. "I think I'm gonna have to start tucking you in every night, baby."

Ella bit her lip, her heart fluttering. She really liked the idea of that.

TWELVE
KING

Fuck, her bed was small.

King sat on the edge, his large frame making the twin-size mattress dip as he watched her snuggle deeper under the covers. She looked so soft, so utterly Little, her long lashes fluttering as she peeked up at him through heavy lids. Her stuffed bunny was tucked under one arm, her nightie slightly oversized on her petite frame, making her look even more delicate.

He reached down, smoothing the blanket over her before his voice dropped to a gentle murmur.

"Do you have a paci, Little one?"

Ella's cheeks burned pink, and her fingers twitched as they rested against the blanket. Slowly, she lifted a hand, pointing at the nightstand.

King followed her gaze, pulling the drawer open. Inside, there was a neat row of pacifiers in a variety of soft pastels decorated with tiny designs—polka dots, rainbows, bunnies. Of course, she would have a bunny pacifier. Something about seeing them nestled in the drawer, knowing she used them, maybe even needed them, made his chest tighten with warmth.

He picked one up, a pink pacifier with a small, white plastic bow on the front of it, and held it out to her.

She hesitated, her blush deepening as her fingers curled around it. For a second, she looked like she might change her mind, but then, after a shallow breath, she brought it to her lips and slipped it into her mouth.

King swallowed hard, watching the way her lips closed around the silicone.

Perfect. So damn perfect.

His hand reached up, brushing a few strands of hair from her face before tucking her bunny closer into her chest. "Sleep, baby," he murmured. "I'll text you in the morning. I want to see you tomorrow."

Ella blinked up at him sleepily, her eyes trusting, warm.

His heart clenched. He was falling for her, and he knew it. And he wasn't going to fight it because no one had ever made him *feel* like Ella did.

Leaning down, he pressed a soft kiss to her forehead, lingering a second longer than he should have.

Then, with a final glance, he stood and forced himself to leave.

The drive back to the clubhouse was quiet, but his head wasn't.

Ella.

Everything about her consumed him. The way she looked up at him with big, trusting eyes, how she blushed when he teased her, watching her slip so effortlessly into Little Space with him.

He'd hated leaving her. For a moment, he'd considered crashing on her small couch so he could be near her, but he didn't want to overwhelm her yet.

One thing he already knew, though.

She was *his.*

Or at least, she would be.

Soon.

He pulled into the lot, parking his truck outside the clubhouse. But as soon as he killed the engine, another set of headlights turned into the lot behind him. He didn't recognize the car and immediately went on alert. It was awfully late for a visitor to show up.

The second the car stopped, the door swung open, and Janelle stepped out, her heels clicking against the pavement.

His blood ran cold, and he ground his molars together.

"What the hell are you doing here?" King snapped, stepping out of his truck, his fists clenched at his sides.

Janelle scoffed, crossing her arms under her chest as she tossed her dark hair over her shoulder. "Relax, Daddy. I just happened to see you pulling in."

"Bullshit. And don't fucking call me that." His voice was sharp, cutting. "Are you following me, Janelle?"

She rolled her eyes. "Of course not. But I did hear you've been spending time with some pathetic little girl. Took her to the steakhouse tonight, apparently." Her lip curled. "Seriously? That's what you want? Someone like *her?*"

His muscles tensed. "You don't get to ask me that." His tone was low and dangerous. "Now get the fuck out of here before I call the cops and report you for harassment."

Janelle let out a sharp laugh, but there was an edge of desperation in it. "You're really choosing *her* over me?"

"Without a second thought."

Her face twisted in anger, but King was done.

"Get the fuck out of here, Janelle. And stay the hell out of my life. We're over, have been for a long time, and that is never going to change," he snapped.

Turning on his heel, he stalked toward the clubhouse, shoving open the door without looking back.

He didn't need to.

Because Janelle?

She was nothing but a nightmare from the past.

But Ella?

Ella was his future. And she was quickly becoming his everything.

King leaned against the counter, phone in hand as he stared at the screen. His fingers hovered over the keyboard for a second before he typed out a message.

> King: Morning, Little one. Come spend the day with me?

It only took a minute before the dots appeared, then her reply popped up.

> Ella: Spend the day with you... doing what?

> King: Playing with the other Littles. Having fun. Being taken care of.

> Ella: Okay. I'd like that.

A slow grin spread across his face.

He pushed off the counter and walked into the common room, where a few Littles were already gathered, sprawled across the couches with coloring books and cartoons playing softly in the background.

"Hey, rugrats," he called out, getting their attention. "Ella's coming over in a little while."

A chorus of excited squeals erupted as Remi, Harper, and some of the others sat up, their eyes wide with excitement.

"Really?" Remi bounced in place. "She's coming to play?"

"Yep."

Harper waggled her eyebrows at him. "Is she your Little?"

King huffed out a laugh, shaking his head. "Not yet."

"But you want her to be," Molly chimed in with a knowing grin.

King felt a flicker of warmth in his chest. *More than anything.*

"That's up to Ella," he said, keeping his voice steady even though hope clung to him.

Harper crossed her arms, nodding sagely. "Well, we already decided. We like her. So she should be yours."

King chuckled. "Glad I have your approval."

Remi clapped her hands. "We should have a picnic when she gets here."

"I was already planning on making sandwiches and snacks. You can set everything up outside while I take care of the food," King told them.

With that settled, the Littles scattered to start preparing for their picnic, and King headed into the kitchen. He pulled out bread, lunch meat, and various snacks, getting everything out before rolling his sleeves up to get to work.

A few minutes later, Doc walked in, his expression easy as he grabbed a knife and started helping slice the fruit. The men all helped each other out around the club, both with chores and taking care of each other's women. The entire club was a family of its own.

King gave him a nod of appreciation before Doc spoke.

"Saw Janelle follow you through the compound gates last night," he noted casually.

King's jaw tightened, but he kept his hands steady as he spread mayo onto a slice of bread. "Yeah, she showed up."

Doc exhaled, shaking his head. "That woman's bad news, King. You know that. People like her don't just let things go."

King let out a low grunt. "I made it real fucking clear to her last night that I want nothing to do with her."

"You sure she got the message?"

King paused, his grip tightening around the butter knife for a second before he forced himself to relax. "I hope so, but if not, she will."

Doc didn't say anything for a moment, then gave a short nod. "Just be careful. You've got something good with Ella. Don't let Janelle mess that up."

King's stomach tightened at the thought of Janelle doing anything to hurt Ella. He wouldn't let it happen. Not now. Not ever.

"I won't," he said firmly.

Doc clapped him on the shoulder before moving to pack up the food.

King rolled his neck and exhaled slowly.

Ella would be here soon.

And he'd be damned if anything—*or anyone*—got in the way of what they were building.

King stood outside the clubhouse, arms crossed as he waited for Ella. The moment her car pulled up, his lips curled into a grin, anticipation thrumming through his chest. As soon as she stepped out, he closed the distance between them, wrapping his arms around her and pulling her in for a hug. She melted into him easily, her small frame fitting perfectly against his.

"I missed you," he said, pressing a lingering kiss to the top of her head before tilting her chin up and brushing a soft kiss against her lips.

Ella blushed, her fingers tightening in the fabric of his shirt. "I missed you, too," she admitted, her voice shy. "Even though it hasn't even been that long."

King grinned, brushing a stray lock of hair away from her cheek. "That so, Little one?"

She nodded, chewing her lip before glancing up at him with uncertainty in her eyes. "I've never felt like this before. I don't know if we're moving too fast. I was kind of panicking this morning."

King tightened his grip on her waist, keeping her close. "We *are* moving fast," he admitted. "But I don't care. Not if it's what we both want."

He cupped her cheek, rubbing his thumb over her warm skin. "I want this. I want *you*. And I want to be your Daddy. Not just that. I want to be your partner, too."

Ella's breath hitched, her wide eyes locking onto his. Her lips parted, and just as she was about to speak, they were interrupted.

"Ella!"

A chorus of excited squeals rang out as Carlee, Ivy, and Remi came skipping over, their faces bright with excitement.

"Come play with us," Ivy pleaded, bouncing on her toes.

Remi grabbed Ella's hand, tugging her toward the clubhouse. "We're gonna have a picnic."

Ella hesitated, her eyes flicking to King, uncertainty flashing across her face.

King chuckled, brushing his knuckles over her jaw before nodding toward the girls. "Go on, Little one. Have fun."

Her lips curled into a soft smile, and with one last glance at him, she let the girls pull her away, their giggles filling the air as they hurried to the picnic they'd set up by the oak tree.

It was going to be a good day.

THIRTEEN
ELLA

Ella skipped off with the other Littles, feeling lighter than she had in days. As she moved away, King's deep voice rumbled behind her.

"Be good, Little one."

She glanced back over her shoulder, her smile bright and playful. "I *always* am," she teased before hurrying to catch up with the others.

His laughter made her grin even wider.

Once they were sitting by a large tree, Carlee, Ivy, Harper, Remi, and the rest of the Littles surrounded her while they passed out sandwiches and juice boxes, their eyes sparkling with curiosity.

"Okay, spill," Ivy demanded, plopping onto the ground and crossing her arms. "How was your date?"

Ella's cheeks burned as she tucked a strand of hair behind her ear. "It was… really nice," she admitted, smiling to herself at the memory of the restaurant and drive-in.

Harper gasped. "Is he your Daddy yet?"

Ella shook her head quickly, though her stomach fluttered. "No… but he said he wants to be."

That earned a chorus of squeals from the group.

"Then what are you waiting for?" Remi grinned, nudging her playfully.

Ella shrugged, biting her lip. "I don't know. It's just... a big step, you know?"

Ivy rolled her eyes, leaning back on the blanket dramatically. "Girl, please. We all knew he was gonna claim you the second he laid eyes on you."

Ella giggled, unable to argue. King had made his intentions pretty obvious. And she loved that he was so vocal about it.

Her cheeks burned the entire time they ate as she thought about his words.

I want this. I want you. And I want to be your Daddy. Not just that. I want to be your partner, too.

Everything he was offering seemed so amazing. She'd never thought she'd find a Daddy, let alone one who she liked so much.

"All right," Carlee clapped her hands together once they'd finished their lunch. "What are we doing today?"

"Ooh! Let's play hide-and-seek!" Harper suggested excitedly, bouncing on her toes.

A round of excited agreements followed, and within seconds, they were choosing someone to be "it." When Remi volunteered, everyone scattered, squealing and giggling as they ran off to find hiding spots.

Harper grabbed Ella's hand, and the two of them dashed across the compound until they spotted a thick bush near the side of one of the buildings. They ducked behind it, crouching low as they tried to stifle their laughter.

Ella pressed a finger to her lips, eyes twinkling with mischief. "Shh! She'll totally find us if we keep giggling."

Harper clamped her hands over her mouth, her whole body shaking with silent laughter. Ella giggled, too. She hadn't played like this before. Mostly because she had never really had any friends in New York.

And in that moment, as Remi rounded the bush and found

them, Ella knew she'd made the best decision of her life by moving to Shadowridge.

The game had gone on for hours, filled with giggles, whispered plans, and frantic scrambles to avoid being found. Ella had lost count of how many rounds they'd played, but she wasn't ready to stop. Not when she was having so much fun.

Crouched behind an old stack of wooden crates with Remi and Harper, she tried to steady her breathing, listening as the Daddies started calling them.

"All right, Littles, the game's over. Come get something to drink and take a break." Doc's voice rang out across the yard.

Ella glanced at the other two, biting her lip.

"We should go…" she whispered.

Remi snorted. "Or—hear me out—we don't."

Harper gasped with delight. "Oh, we should totally make them find us."

Ella's stomach twisted with both excitement and nerves. "Won't that… you know… make them mad?"

Remi waggled her brows. "No. They know we're somewhere within the compound, so we're safe. Besides, it'll be fun to see what happens."

Harper grinned. "They're used to us being naughty. It gives them a reason to discipline us."

Ella hesitated, but the idea intrigued her. Would King really discipline her if she pushed the boundary? She wasn't sure, but her curiosity outweighed her nerves, so she stayed put.

Outside, the men's voices grew louder and sharper.

"Girls!" Doc called, sounding much less amused.

"Not funny anymore, Littles!" Kade's voice followed.

Ella gulped, eyes darting to Remi and Harper, but they were grinning like they had no regrets.

Then she heard *his* voice.

"Ella."

Her stomach flipped.

"I'm going to count to three," King warned, his deep voice laced with authority. "If you don't come out by three, Little girl, you're going to be in trouble."

Ella's breath caught, her heart hammering against her ribs.

Harper giggled quietly. "Oh, this is gonna be interesting."

Remi giggled. "Told you this was a great idea."

Ella's whole body tingled as King started counting.

"One."

She squeezed her hands into fists, fighting the urge to leap up and obey him.

"Two."

Harper whispered, "You sure about this?"

No. Absolutely not.

"Three."

Ella clenched her eyes shut, bracing for whatever was coming.

The silence stretched for a second before heavy footsteps moved toward them. Then, suddenly—

"There you are," King's stern voice said.

Ella's eyes flew open to find King, Doc, and Kade standing over them, their arms crossed and their expressions firm.

"Up. *Now*," Kade ordered, his gaze fixed on Remi.

Doc shook his head at Harper, sighing. "You never learn, do you, baby girl?"

Harper giggled, utterly unrepentant.

Ella, on the other hand, swallowed hard as King's intense gaze locked onto hers.

"You've got some nerve, dollface," he rumbled. "Get inside."

Her stomach flipped as she scrambled to her feet, suddenly wondering if she really had thought this through.

FOURTEEN
KING

King's grip was firm but not rough as he guided Ella through the clubhouse, his jaw tight. Kade and Doc led their Littles in the opposite direction, leaving King alone with Ella as he pushed open the door to his small apartment.

The moment they were inside, he turned and shut the door behind them. Ella stood there, her hands twisting together, her bottom lip caught between her teeth as she peered up at him, looking uncertain.

Part of him was pleased. Pleased that she felt safe enough to push the boundaries, to test the limits of their growing dynamic. It told him she trusted him. But another part of him, the part still rattled by the sharp bite of fear that had clenched his chest when she hadn't come when called, needed Ella to understand that what she'd done wasn't going to be ignored.

He exhaled slowly, running a hand down his face before leveling her with a steady look. "Go and stand in the corner."

Ella's eyes widened, her lips parting slightly in surprise.

King arched a brow, crossing his arms over his broad chest. "That wasn't a suggestion, Little girl."

Her shoulders slumped slightly, but she obeyed him, shuffling over to the empty corner of the room. She hesitated once more before finally turning to face the wall, her hands clasped in front of her.

King let a beat of silence settle before he spoke. "I want you to listen to me carefully, dollface. I know you were playing with the others. I know you were having fun. And I love seeing you happy. But when I called for you and told you I was going to count, I wasn't just being bossy—I was worried."

Ella didn't move, but he saw her tiny shoulders tense.

"You might not officially be my Little girl yet, but that doesn't change the fact that when you're here, I consider you mine to protect. That means I'm *responsible* for you. And if something were to happen because you didn't listen—" He exhaled sharply, forcing down the knot in his chest. "I can't let that slide, baby. I need to know that when I tell you to do something for your safety, you're going to listen. I'm really strict when it comes to safety because, in my line of work, I see a lot. More than any person ever should. So I worry more than some of the other Daddies. I don't want anything to happen to you."

The room was quiet except for the sound of Ella's breathing, and then—

A sniffle.

King's chest ached, but he knew he couldn't give in yet. She needed to learn.

He let her stand there for a few more minutes, letting his words sink in. Letting her feel the weight of them.

Finally, he said, "Come here, Little one."

She turned slowly, her face pink, her big eyes glossy with unshed tears. His heart squeezed, but he kept his expression steady as he patted his thighs. As soon as she was close, he reached for her.

King kept his hands firm but gentle on Ella's hips, holding her steady as she stood between his thighs. Her red-rimmed eyes were sad from her timeout, her small sniffs tugging at something deep inside him. But he had to stay firm—this was important.

"I want to be your Daddy," he told her firmly.

Ella's breath caught, and she nodded immediately, like she'd been waiting for him to say it.

His lips twitched into a small smile. "And I want you to be my girlfriend, too. Do you want that?"

Another nod. "Yes," she whispered.

He ran his hands up and down her sides. "Good girl." Then his expression turned serious. "But being your Daddy means I have responsibilities, baby. My job is to keep you safe, to make sure you follow the rules and obey. When I told you to come out and you didn't, that was naughty."

She bit her lip, her hands fidgeting at her sides.

He gave her a pointed look. "You disobeyed me, and worse, you made me worry. That means there are consequences." He let his words settle before continuing, "You deserve a spanking."

Ella's breath hitched, her cheeks turning pink, but she didn't argue.

"I'm going to put you over my knee and spank your bottom," he told her resolutely. "And once it's done, it's done. All is forgiven. You'll be able to go back to playing with your friends, and we'll move on."

She sniffled, but after a moment, she gave a tiny nod.

King reached up, cupping her cheek, his thumb swiping a stray tear away. "Later, we'll go over your rules and boundaries together. But for now, let's get this over with."

FIFTEEN
ELLA

Ella's heart pounded as King gently guided her over his knee, her small hands bracing against the couch as her stomach pressed into his strong thighs. She felt completely vulnerable in a way that made her squirm.

"You know why this is happening, don't you, baby?"

She nodded against the cushions, her breath coming in pants. "Yes, Daddy."

The realization of what she'd called him hit her, but it had come so easily. So natural. It felt right.

"Good girl," he said softly. "Do you remember what your safeword is to make things come to a halt if you need them to?"

"Yes. Red."

"Good. You can say it any time if things become too much or painful. Since this is your first spanking, I'm going to take it easy on you, but you can still safeword at any time."

Her chest ached, and his gentle reassurances made her feel even worse for being so naughty. He was being so sweet and taking such good care of her, and all she'd been was a brat.

His hand rubbed slow, comforting circles over her bottom before he lifted it. A sharp smack landed on her right cheek, making her gasp.

Before she could process it, another came on the left, the sting sinking in deep.

"Ow—Daddy!" she whined, kicking her legs.

King simply tightened his grip around her waist, keeping her pinned over his lap.

"You were naughty, Little girl. Hiding from me. Making me worry."

Smack. Smack. Smack.

Ella let out a soft cry, trying to wiggle away from the firm, steady rhythm of his hand, but he didn't let up. Each strike sent a warm burn through her, making her bottom feel hotter by the second.

"I-I'm sorry," she cried, gripping the couch cushion.

"I know, baby," King said, but he didn't stop. "But I need to make sure you remember."

Tears welled in her eyes as the spanking continued, her legs kicking helplessly.

"I do! I remember! I won't do it again!" she sobbed.

"I hope you won't," he replied as he tucked his hand into the back of her leggings and panties.

As he pulled the fabric down, baring her bottom, she whimpered. She was sure he could see everything, including her pussy and the damp spot on her panties. If he did, he didn't say anything about it. Instead, he carried on with her spanking, this time on her already hot bottom.

"If I call for you and tell you I'm going to count, that means serious business, dollface. I expect you to stop playing and come to me."

Sniffling, she cried out over and over while kicking her feet wildly. She'd read about spankings and even fantasized about them, but she'd never experienced one. It was terrible. Her butt was on fire, and her chest ached with a sadness that she hadn't expected. She'd disappointed him, and she hated that. It was the last thing she wanted.

"I'm sorry, Daddy," she wailed loudly, collapsing over his

lap. "I won't do it ever again."

Tears trailed down her cheeks, and even though she was sure she would never sit again, her heart felt full in a way she hadn't expected.

King landed a final, firm swat before he was lifting her, pulling her into his chest. The moment she was curled against him, she buried her face against his neck, crying softly. He held her tightly, one hand rubbing slow, soothing circles down her spine.

"You did so good for me, sweetheart," he murmured, his lips pressing into her hair. "Took your punishment like a good girl."

Ella hiccupped, snuggling closer as he rocked her. The warmth of his body surrounded her, making her feel safe despite her sore bottom.

After a few minutes, he pulled back just enough to tilt her chin up, his dark eyes filled with nothing but warmth. "It's over now, Little one. All is forgiven."

Then he leaned down and kissed her softly, his lips brushing hers in a way that made her stomach flutter. When he broke away, he reached into his pocket and pulled out a pacifier, offering it to her. She hesitated for a moment before taking it, slipping it between her lips. The familiar, calming motion of sucking settled something deep inside her, and she melted against him.

King held her close, stroking her hair while she relaxed into his arms, her sniffles fading. She knew she'd been naughty, but in his embrace, she felt nothing but peace and something she wasn't expecting.

She felt loved.

Ella sighed in contentment as she curled up against King's chest, his arms wrapped securely around her as they relaxed on his couch. The low hum of the movie played in the background, but she wasn't paying attention. It was hard to focus on anything when King's steady heartbeat thumped beneath her ear, his warmth surrounding her like a protective cocoon.

He had her tucked between his legs, her body cradled against his, and every so often, he ran his fingers lazily through her hair, making her shiver. She felt safe. Secure. Like she belonged here, in his arms.

"You comfy, baby?" he murmured, his lips pressing lightly against her head.

She nodded, snuggling even closer. "Mm-hmm. Really comfy."

His deep chuckle rumbled against her cheek. "Good. You better be. I like having you here."

Her cheeks warmed, but she didn't respond. Mostly because she liked being there too much, and it scared her a bit. Everything with King was moving so fast, yet it felt so right.

They stayed like that for hours, King occasionally shifting to adjust her or whisper in her ear, but for the most part, they just existed together, wrapped up in each other.

After her punishment had ended and she had calmed down, he told her she could go back to playing with the other girls, but she wanted to stay with him. So he turned on a movie for them while he cuddled and babied her.

When dinnertime rolled around, King finally moved, stretching beneath her before shifting her off his lap. "Come on, Little one. Let's get some food in that tummy."

She let out a small whine at the loss of his warmth but let him pull her to her feet. Hand in hand, he led her out of his apartment and into the common area where the rest of the club members and Littles were gathering for dinner.

The moment they stepped into the dining room, Ella hesitated, feeling a little overwhelmed by the lively energy of the clubhouse. The tables were filled with people chatting, laughing, and teasing one another. For a second, she thought about asking King if they could eat alone. Ever since her spanking, she'd felt extra Little and clingy.

But he didn't give her the chance. He led her straight to the food, grabbing two plates and filling them up. When she sat down, she winced as her bottom came into contact with the chair, but one look at Harper and she knew she wasn't alone. The other girls had gotten their bottoms spanked, too. And that kind of comforted her.

As soon as King sat next to her, she expected him to slide a plate in front of her, but instead, he scooted his chair closer and held up a forkful of food.

She blinked at him. "You're... gonna feed me?"

King smirked. "That a problem, dollface?"

Her cheeks burned as she glanced around, suddenly hyper-aware of how many people were in the room. But then, her eyes landed on Ivy, snuggled in Steele's lap as he fed her. Remi was curled up beside Kade, giggling as he held a spoon to her lips.

Ella's stomach flipped. This wasn't weird in the compound. This was normal.

Slowly, she turned back to King, pausing for a second before parting her lips and letting him slide the bite into her mouth.

"Good girl," he murmured, his voice low and warm.

She shivered, chewing slowly as he continued to feed her, his eyes never leaving hers. Every bite he gave her, every soft murmur of praise, sent little flutters through her belly.

By the time dinner was over, she wasn't even thinking about being embarrassed anymore. She just felt... cherished. Taken care of.

Ella sat back in her chair, her belly pleasantly full from the meal King had fed her. The others were chatting around the table, but King stood up and took her hand, leading her toward his apartment. She followed willingly, feeling a sense of contentment that only seemed to grow the more time she spent with him.

Once they were inside, King smiled down at her. "Stay here, baby. I'll be right back."

Ella nodded as he disappeared from the apartment. She was a little lost without him by her side, but she settled onto the couch, curling up with one of the throw pillows. The soft fabric and the quiet atmosphere of his personal space put her at ease, like this was where she was supposed to be.

Her thoughts wandered while she waited. She couldn't help but smile, recalling how King had fed her earlier. The tenderness in his actions had been so... caring. She'd never felt anything like it before, and it made her feel warm and cherished in a way she didn't know was possible.

After what felt like only a few moments, she heard King's footsteps approaching.

He stepped into the doorway, arms loaded with an assortment of new toys and Little items. Her heart fluttered as she took in the sight—a colorful collection of plush toys, a playful rattle, a doll, and even a few items she hadn't seen before.

With a soft giggle, she asked, "Where did you get all that?"

King's smile was warm as he stepped closer. "We have a shared closet for Little items. The other Daddies and I always make sure we have extras ready when a new Little comes to the compound."

Her fingers danced over each object as she examined them one by one. "I can't believe you have all of this," she murmured, barely able to contain her excitement.

One of the toys she studied was a pink stuffed bear wearing a tiny T-shirt, which had the logo of their club printed on the front. It was instantly her new favorite stuffy.

King's eyes crinkled at the corners. "I knew you'd like them. They're all for you."

When her hand brushed against a baby bottle, she lifted it, her gaze meeting his with a questioning look.

"Do you… like this?" she asked timidly.

King's gaze softened even more. "At bedtime and nap time, I'd like to bottle feed you… If that's not a hard limit for you."

Her cheeks flushed as she shook her head eagerly. "No, I think I might like that."

A warm surge of relief and excitement coursed through her as she continued to inspect every new toy. "I can't believe you guys have a closet of Little stuff. It's so thoughtful."

King reached out and tucked a stray lock of hair behind her ear. "We want every Little who comes here to have things to make them feel comfortable and to be taken care of."

After she had taken in every item with bright, childlike fascination, King stepped closer and cupped her chin. "Will you stay the night with me?"

Without hesitation, her heart fluttering, she whispered, "Yes."

King's smile deepened, and he excused himself, disappearing from the apartment. Moments later, he reappeared carrying an armful of neatly folded clothes. New garments just for Littles. As he spread them out on a chair, Ella's eyes sparkled at the soft, pastel fabrics and delicate designs. Among the items was a pair of training panties for bedtime.

Her cheeks burned as she stared at them. "Oh… these are so pretty," she managed to say, though she sounded nervous.

King chuckled gently. "I thought you might like them. I want you to have everything that makes you feel Little and special."

"Thank you, Daddy," she said quietly. "It's all so new and a little scary, but I… I trust you."

"I know it's new for you, baby, but I promise—everything we do, every new experience, is meant to make you feel safe and cherished."

She nibbled on her bottom lip as she examined the clothes. "I want to be your Little girl, and I want to learn, to experience everything with you."

King's smile widened. "We'll take it one step at a time. Tonight, let's start with trying on these clothes."

"Okay."

He reached out and lightly brushed his thumb over her hand. "I want to give you all the firsts you deserve and to care for you as my Little girl and my woman."

A flutter of excitement and warmth coursed through her at his words.

"I want that, too," she replied softly.

King's eyes held hers, and for a moment, everything around them faded away. "Come on then, baby. Let's get you changed into your new nightie and panties."

Ella smiled shyly. "Okay, Daddy."

The word came out more naturally than she expected. Everything with King felt so natural. Like they were meant to be.

SIXTEEN
KING

King slowly removed Ella's clothes, piece by piece, letting her get used to him touching her so intimately. She shivered and bit her bottom lip but didn't push him away, tell him to stop, or use her safeword. He didn't let his hands linger, though his eyes were another story.

Her rosy, pink nipples were practically begging for his mouth. It wasn't the time for that, though. Right now was about her being Little and learning to trust and allow him to take care of her. To let her be comforted, knowing she could be her truest self with him, and he would love every second of being her Daddy.

Sex would come later. And it would be amazing and worth the wait. King already knew Ella was his future. He was sure of it down to his bones. So, he would be patient and take things one step at a time. He was pretty sure she wasn't a virgin, but he was also pretty sure that whatever experiences she'd had with men had been lacking and having a caretaker like him was totally new to her.

He dropped the nightie over her head, smiling at the two bunnies on the front with the words *Best Bunnies* printed on it.

"I need a bunch more bunnies on here, Daddy," she

murmured as she looked down at it. "I finally have friends. Lots of them."

"Yeah, dollface. You do have lots of them."

Warmth spread through him as a lump formed in his throat. He hated that she'd grown up without something so important. Her parents might have been loving and kind, but he wished they would have realized what she was missing. He was glad that they hadn't given her a hard time about moving to Shadowridge because this was the best place for his sweet girl. She would be surrounded by friends here, and she'd be safe with him and the rest of the MC. Part of him wondered if she missed her parents. Even though he didn't get to see his own as much as he'd like, he couldn't imagine living on the other side of the country from them.

"Hold my shoulders and step out of your panties, baby," he instructed.

She did as she was told. Not that it surprised him. Littles with tender bottoms usually behaved *especially* well for a while.

When he slid the new training panties up her legs and adjusted them over her waist, he caught a glimpse of her bare pussy, her lips shining with her dew. His cock ached, but he ignored it. He loved that her body was having the same reactions as his. When the time came, he would make sure he showed her how much he loved it.

She squirmed slightly, probably trying to get used to the padding between her legs, which was there to absorb anything in the event of an accident. They hadn't discussed her wearing diapers, but King got the feeling that Ella went really Little when she was in that headspace, so he went with his gut on what she might like. And based on her soft smile and twinkling eyes, he was pretty sure he'd guessed right.

"Dollface," he began softly, his gaze locked on hers as if trying to imprint every detail of her face, "we need to talk about the rules of our relationship."

Ella shifted closer, her eyes wide and attentive.

King took a slow breath and continued, "When we're alone or even at the clubhouse with the others, I want you to be completely dependent on me. Trust me for everything. I want to help you with eating, using the bathroom, getting dressed, bath time... and every other thing I can help with."

He paused, watching as her pupils dilated ever so slightly—a silent affirmation that his words were stirring something deep within her. Encouraged, he pressed on. "I have specific rules, baby. Rules I expect you to follow to keep you safe and cared for."

King leaned in a little closer, his voice dropping even further. "For instance, when I'm around, you'll ask me before doing certain things like going outside or getting snacks so I can ensure you're not eating candy salad all the time. Before making plans, you'll need to check with me, and you'll let me take care of you intimately. Which means things like diapering you before bedtime or taking your temperature in your bottom."

He searched her face, and when he saw a soft nod and a flicker of understanding, he felt his resolve strengthen.

After a measured pause, he continued, "I need to know if you have any hard limits. Anything you're not comfortable with?"

The room was silent for a long, weighted moment. King's heart pounded as he scanned her face for any sign of hesitation or doubt.

Finally, in a small, quiet voice, she replied, "I... I don't think there are any, Daddy, but I also don't have a lot of experience, so I can't say for sure."

A small smile tugged at King's lips as he reached out to gently stroke a stray hair away from her forehead. "Okay, baby," he said softly. "We'll adjust as we go, but remember: if something ever feels like too much, you tell me. This is about keeping you safe and making sure you feel cared for. Red will always be your safeword, and you are allowed to say it at any time. Understand?"

"Yes, Daddy. I understand."

King's heart swelled at her response. "Remember, we can make adjustments at any time. You can talk to me about anything anytime, and we will make changes. It's my job to make sure you feel safe, and I take that very seriously. Tomorrow we can write out a list of rules and talk about them more in-depth."

Without breaking eye contact, Ella nodded again, smiling at him. He reached for her and picked her up effortlessly, and she immediately wrapped herself around him. Leaving her dirty clothes in a pile on the floor, he carried her into the bathroom and set her in front of the toilet. When he reached for her training panties and pulled them down, he half expected her to push him away, but instead, she blushed bright red and wiggled in place.

"Good girl. Sit and go potty. I'm going to get your toothbrush ready for you."

He intentionally turned on the vanity faucet and made himself busy, letting her get used to having him in her space while she did something very personal. There would be many awkward and embarrassing moments as they got to know each other, but that was half the fun.

As soon as she finished, he let her clean herself up and pull up her panties, then he waited for her to come to the sink and wash her hands. The entire time they watched each other in the mirror, the air between them was electrified. Just looking at her got his heart racing.

"Open," he instructed after she dried her hands.

She eyed the toothbrush but obeyed, and he brushed her teeth. It was a small thing that felt so damn big. So special. All he could think about was if she would be willing to give up her tiny house and come and live at the compound with him. Hell, he'd figure out a way to fit in the twin bed at her place with her if he had to so he could spend every night with her. It didn't matter where they were as long as they were together.

King had never considered himself as obsessive as some of

his brothers, but now he was starting to second guess that because he wanted to be with Ella every spare minute.

"It's bedtime, dollface."

Ella made a face and sighed, but she followed him into the bedroom. He placed his hands on her shoulders and pointed toward the couch, where the toys were piled.

"Go grab something to sleep with." He patted her bottom, and she looked back at him with a wide, sleepy grin.

When she brought the stuffed Shadowridge Guardians bear over to the bed, he wasn't surprised. He noticed how bright her eyes had gotten when she'd seen it. Fucking adorable.

"Are you going to come to bed with me?" she asked.

King pulled the covers up to her chin and leaned over, resting a hand on either side of her head. "I'm going to shower, and then I'll get into bed with you. Here, suck on your paci, and I'll be out in no time."

As soon as he slid the paci between her lips, her eyes closed, and he had no doubt she'd be passed out by the time he returned. It had been a big day for his Little girl, and she was exhausted. So was he, but there was no way he'd be able to sleep until he did something about his painful erection, so a shower came first, and then he'd snuggle his girl all night long.

SEVENTEEN
ELLA

Ella drove through Shadowridge with what felt like a permanent smile. The early afternoon sun glinted off her windshield as she navigated from one stop to the next. Her route took her to the police station, the local hospital, and finally, the food bank, meticulously taking inventory for the food drive from the various collection points.

Her mind wandered as she scribbled notes on her clipboard at each stop while constantly thinking about the tender moments she'd shared with King over the past few weeks. His gentle guidance, his protective reminders, and the way his soft-spoken words made her feel so special. The thought of being cared for by him in every tiny detail filled her with a warm, secure happiness that she'd never known before. Shadowridge, with its close-knit community and laid-back charm, had become Ella's home. Here she could be her most authentic self without the worry of ruining her parents' reputation or becoming a laughingstock of their social circle.

As she drove along the streets, lined with old oak trees and pastel-painted storefronts, a pang of longing tugged at her heart. Despite loving Shadowridge, part of her still missed her parents.

She'd texted them occasionally, but it wasn't the same as hearing their voices or feeling their hugs.

With her lunch break approaching, Ella pulled over at a small park with a weathered picnic table and a few shady trees. Taking a deep breath, she reached for her phone and dialed her mom.

After a few rings, her mother's warm, bright voice filled the line. "Ella! Oh, my darling, it's so good to hear from you. We miss you terribly."

"I miss you both," she admitted softly. "I'm really happy here in Shadowridge, but sometimes I think I'm a little homesick."

Her mother's tone softened. "Your father and I are always here for you, sweetheart. Your father sends his love, too. Hold on, he's telling me to put it on speaker."

Just then, her father's familiar baritone came on the line. "Hey, kiddo. I just wanted to tell you I love you and miss you. Remember, no matter where you are, you're always home with us."

Hearing those words, Ella felt a bittersweet mix of comfort and longing. The warmth of their voices wrapped around her like a cozy blanket, even as she sat in a parking lot surrounded by the place she now considered home. She closed her eyes for a moment, letting the love of her parents soothe her homesick heart.

"Ella, are you okay, sweetheart? Remember, you can always move back if things get too overwhelming," her mother said.

Ella hesitated, her thoughts swirling with both excitement and apprehension.

Finally, after a deep, steadying breath, she spoke. "I... I've met someone."

Her mother's tone brightened instantly. "Oh, really? Tell me about him, darling."

Ella's cheeks flushed a deep rose as she carefully explained, "His name is King. He's a firefighter, and... he's incredibly caring." She paused for a moment. "He takes care of me in ways I never thought possible."

Her father's voice, warm and full of pride, joined in. "A fire-fighter, you say? That's wonderful, kiddo. We're so happy for you."

A brief silence stretched over the line before her mother ventured, "Ella, does King know about your... Little side?"

Ella gasped.

Had she heard that correctly? She'd never shared her Little side with anyone in New York.

Her mother laughed softly. "Don't sound so surprised, honey. We've always known. We understood that you needed a way to escape and find comfort in your Little headspace, especially with all the stress of New York. We knew life here was hard on you. It's hard on us sometimes, too. There were times we talked about moving away to start afresh where nobody knew us. We couldn't be prouder of you for doing that. No matter what, we've always loved you, just the way you are."

Tears welled in Ella's eyes as she absorbed the sincerity of their words. "I... I really miss you both."

Her father's tone grew even softer. "We miss you every day, kiddo. Just knowing you're happy means the world to us. And we hope to meet King soon. To see the man who's taking such good care of our daughter."

There was another pause, and then her mother added, "Remember, darling, you can always call us if you feel alone or need anything. We're here, no matter what."

Ella's heart swelled as a painful lump formed in her throat. "I'll keep in touch, Mom."

After exchanging goodbyes, the call ended, and she was left in the quiet of her car. Ella felt a surge of overwhelming emotion. The mixture of her parents' love and the hope of a future with King swirled inside her, and before she could stop herself, tears of happiness streamed down her face.

Ella wiped her cheeks, taking a few deep breaths to steady herself. The emotions of the conversation with her parents still lingered. She couldn't believe they knew about her Little side.

And they accepted it. They understood it. They understood her.

After letting out a deep sigh, she started her car.

She wanted to see her Daddy. To hug and kiss him.

As she pulled away from the park, a shiver crawled down her spine.

The uneasy feeling prickled at the back of her neck. It felt like she was being watched. She shook it off, gripping the wheel tighter as she turned onto Main Street.

But the anxiety didn't go away.

She checked her mirrors. Nothing seemed out of place. Just the usual slow-moving cars, pedestrians walking along the side-walks of Shadowridge's quaint streets, customers popping in and out of the various shops.

The sensation lingered the entire time she drove, but she knew she was being silly. She was just out of sorts after talking to her parents, that was all.

As soon as she pulled into the firehouse lot, the tension in her shoulders eased, and her smile returned because King was standing at the bay opening, almost as if he was expecting her to show up at any time.

EIGHTEEN
KING

King was standing by the entrance of the firehouse when he noticed Ella pull into the parking lot. His heart clenched as he watched her climb out of her car and approach. His sweet girl. Then, as he looked closer, he found himself on alert because her eyes were red and puffy like she'd been crying.

Rushing toward her, he pulled her close. "Baby, are you all right?"

She waved him off with a small, reassuring smile before she wrapped her arms around his waist and hugged him. "I'm fine, Daddy."

When she released him, he studied her and nudged her toward her office. She'd definitely been crying, and he wanted to know why.

Once inside, with the door closed, Ella set her phone on her desk and exhaled slowly. "I just got off the phone with my parents."

King's gaze softened, and he pulled up a chair beside her. "Is everything okay with them?"

Ella hesitated, glancing at her hands. "Mom asked if I was doing okay. They reminded me that I can always come home."

Her voice trailed off, and she paused before continuing in a quieter tone, "It was hard. I don't miss New York at all. I love it here, but I miss *them*."

The room was silent except for the distant hum of activity outside. King's heart ached for Ella. He was relieved that her parents were supportive of her being in Shadowridge and that they cared enough to offer her a way back home, but he hated the thought that she missed them. He reached out, lightly stroking her cheek.

"I'm glad they care, baby," he told her. "I wish I could do something to make your hurt disappear."

Ella looked up into his eyes and smiled. "Thank you," she whispered.

"You're welcome, baby." His fingers still gently grazed her skin. "We'll figure something out. There's no reason we can't make trips to New York every couple of months or they can come here."

Her eyes glistened with tears as she looked up at him. "I feel so lucky to have you."

He let out a deep breath and leaned down so his mouth hovered over hers. "You have no idea how much I feel the same way, dollface."

King leaned against his motorcycle, arms crossed as he watched Ella's car pull into the lot. A slow smile spread across his face, and the second she stepped out, he made his way toward her. Every moment away from her was too long.

"Hey, Little one," he greeted as he wrapped an arm around her waist, pulling her into his chest before pressing a deep, lingering kiss on her lips.

Ella giggled against his mouth, her small hands pressing against his chest as if to steady herself.

"Hi, Daddy," she murmured once he pulled back, her cheeks already pink from his attention.

King cupped her face, running his thumb along the softness of her skin. Something inside him twisted with a deep possessiveness that he couldn't deny. He wanted her. *Needed* her. "Are you staying the night?"

Ella grinned, nodding. "Yes."

"That's my girl." His smile deepened as his grip on her waist tightened slightly, giving her bottom a smack with his free hand.

She let out a squeal of delight and started to turn toward the clubhouse doors. "Okay, I need to find the girls before book club starts."

But King didn't let her go.

Instead, he pulled her into him, his lips claiming hers once more. One of his hands splayed against her lower back, keeping her flush against him, while the other slid up to tangle in her hair, angling her head just how he wanted.

Ella whimpered, her fingers curling into the fabric of his shirt as she melted into his touch. Her tummy pressed against his hard length, and he groaned into her mouth at the friction.

Still unwilling to release her just yet, King trailed kisses down the side of her face, his lips brushing the delicate skin of her neck.

He nuzzled her, inhaling the faint, sweet scent of her shampoo. "You smell good, baby," he murmured, pressing another kiss beneath her ear. "I bet you taste just as good."

Ella let out a soft, breathy laugh, her hands gripping his arms.

"Daddy, I have to go," she whispered, though she made no real effort to pull away from him.

He chuckled, enjoying the way she shivered beneath his touch. Finally, he loosened his hold, allowing her some space. "All right, Little one," he said, his voice dripping with amusement. "Go on. Have fun with your book club. Enjoy those naughty stories I know you Little girls read."

She stepped back, looking adorably dazed, her lips swollen from his kiss. He was glad he wasn't the only one who was affected. Her pointed nipples and glazed eyes gave away her arousal.

Before she turned, he caught her wrist and gave her a pointed look. "Be good for me, yeah?"

Ella bit her lip, then batted her eyelashes playfully. "Do I get a reward if I'm good?"

He chuckled and arched a brow. "I'll definitely reward you."

"Then I suppose I'll behave," she teased, running her fingers down his chest.

King smirked, squeezing her hand before finally letting her go. "That's my girl."

She turned and hurried into the clubhouse while King stood there watching her, already counting the hours until he had her back in his arms.

NINETEEN
ELLA

Ella curled up on one of the oversized bean-bag chairs in the room she'd started calling the Book Nook, surrounded by Ivy, Remi, Molly, Harper, Carlee, Eden, and the rest of the girls. They were supposed to be reading. Technically, *book club* meant they should at least make an attempt at discussing the novel. Instead, they were giggling uncontrollably, the books lying mostly forgotten in their laps.

"I swear," Remi groaned dramatically, shifting in her seat. "My bottom is *so* sore from the spanking Kade gave me earlier." She pouted, rubbing her backside for emphasis. "And all I did was forget to tell him I was leaving the house. That's not even naughty, right?"

Harper snorted. "I mean... depends. Where were you going?"

Remi muttered something under her breath.

Carlee raised an eyebrow. "What was that?"

Remi crossed her arms. "The ice cream parlor."

The room erupted in laughter.

"Oh, yeah," Molly teased. "Because that's definitely a *necessary trip*."

Remi huffed but grinned. "Well, it felt necessary at the time."

Harper sighed dramatically, flopping back against the couch. "At least you're not being poked and prodded constantly. My Daddy keeps taking my temperature like I'm dying just because I've been tired this week."

Ivy shrugged. "Maybe he's being extra careful. You do tend to forget to take care of yourself."

Harper stuck out her tongue. "Rude."

Eden shook her head, giggling. "He just wants to make sure you're okay, Harp."

Ella smiled, listening to the playful back-and-forth. She felt comfortable here, surrounded by Little friends who got her. She stole a glance toward the common room, where King sat with his club brothers, deep in conversation. Even from across the room, he was a magnet, pulling her attention to him.

She felt herself sigh dreamily.

Ivy must have caught her because she grinned and nudged Ella's knee. "Uh-oh, look at her," she teased. "She's got *that* look."

Ella's face burned as she turned back toward the group. "What look?"

"The *I'm head over heels for my Daddy* look," Remi sing-songed, making the others titter.

Ella groaned. "Oh, my gosh, stop."

"No way," Carlee laughed. "We need to hear how things are going with King."

All eyes turned to Ella. She hesitated, twisting a strand of hair around her finger.

"It's... amazing," she admitted softly. "He's wonderful."

The girls collectively *awwed*, but Ella swallowed, shifting a little. "But... it's also scary."

Eden frowned slightly. "Scary, how?"

Ella exhaled, fidgeting with the hem of her sleeve. "Because I think... I mean, I might... be falling in love with him," she confessed. "But I think it's too soon."

The room went silent for a moment before Ivy scoffed. "Oh, honey. That man *already* loves you."

Ella blinked. "What?"

Harper hummed in agreement. "Everyone can see it. He looks at you like you're sunrise and sunset all wrapped in one."

"You can literally feel the way he hovers over you," Remi added. "Not in a bad way, just... he's *always* aware of where you are, always checking on you."

Carlee grinned. "If you're falling, he's waiting to catch you."

Ella's heart thudded in her chest at their words. Could they be right? Did King already feel the same way she did?

Before she could respond, Eden tilted her head. "How's the food drive going?"

Ella sighed, her excitement dimming slightly. "It's... not going as well as I hoped," she admitted. "The need is way more than Mayor Winslow initially thought, and I'm trying to figure out ways to get extra donations."

The girls exchanged thoughtful glances.

"We can help," Molly offered.

"Yeah," Ivy agreed. "We'll brainstorm some ideas and let you know."

Ella smiled gratefully. "That would mean so much. I just don't want anyone going without, you know?"

"Absolutely. It's an amazing cause. We would love to help in any way we can," Carlee assured her. "We'll figure something out."

As the night wound down, the girls eventually dispersed, all of them eagerly returning to their Daddies who were waiting for them around the clubhouse. Ella stood, stretching, and looked toward King. He was already watching her, his expression patient yet intense.

Her stomach flipped.

Book club may have ended, but she had a feeling the most exciting part of her evening was about to begin.

Ella followed King into his apartment, her heart pounding so hard she swore he could hear it. The door shut behind them, startling her and sealing them into the private space.

Her fingers trembled slightly, her nerves tangling inside her. She knew tonight was different. Knew they were about to take their relationship to a new level. She wanted it, wanted *him*, but fear gnawed at the edges of her excitement. What if she messed up or was terrible at sex? What if she couldn't please him?

King turned to face her, his dark eyes scanning her expression carefully. He could sense her hesitation. He could read her so easily.

"You're nervous," he murmured.

Ella swallowed hard and nodded. "I... I am." She hesitated before admitting, "I'm worried I might be bad at it."

King's brow furrowed slightly. "Why would you think that, baby?"

She shifted on her feet, hugging her arms around herself as she lowered her gaze. "I've only done it once," she confessed. "And it was... rushed. Quick. Not really a positive experience." Her cheeks burned as embarrassment crept in.

For a moment, King didn't move or say anything. Then, slowly, he reached out, his warm, calloused hands settling on her arms, rubbing soothing circles into her skin. His touch was grounding, steady.

"Look at me, Little one."

Ella paused, then lifted her gaze to meet his.

"You don't have to worry about that with me. I don't want to rush anything when it comes to you." His fingers trailed down her arms before his hands settled at her waist, pulling her a little closer. "I'm going to take control, baby. All you need to do is obey me. And if it becomes too much, you say red."

A shiver ran down her spine, her breath hitching at his words and the way he spoke, deep and commanding. She loved this man's confidence.

"Do you trust me?" he asked, his thumb brushing the fabric of her dress.

Ella exhaled shakily, but she didn't hesitate this time. "Yes, Daddy," she whispered.

A slow, proud smile spread across King's face. "Good girl."

Then, he kissed her.

It started softly. Gentle and coaxing, like he was giving her time to adjust. His lips moved against hers, his hands sliding up to frame her face, holding her exactly where he wanted her.

Ella whimpered softly, her body melting against his, her nerves slowly fading as warmth spread through her.

She didn't have to be scared.

Not with King.

He would keep her safe.

Ella melted into the kiss, her hands gingerly resting against his chest. He was slow, deliberate, taking his time with a patient kind of hunger. It was like he had all the time in the world to savor her. And maybe he did.

When he finally pulled back, his breath was warm against her lips. "That's my good girl. Fuck, you taste like candy. If I weren't so focused on something else right now, I'd be questioning how much sugar you ate during book club."

She grinned up at him, glad he wasn't asking because they'd all had more than they should have.

When he traced along her jawline with his thumb, she swallowed hard. "I don't know what I'm supposed to do."

"You don't need to know what to do, dollface. That's my job."

A small whimper escaped her throat as his grip tightened.

His lips found the corner of her mouth, teasing her with feather-light kisses before trailing them down her neck. "All you have to do is listen to me. Obey me. Let me take care of you."

Ella's breath hitched. She could do that.

"Okay."

King hummed his approval. "Good girl. Always my good girl."

His hands slid lower, guiding her backward until her legs hit the edge of his bed. Her heart pounded as she looked up at him, the sheer dominance in his gaze sending a wave of heat through her.

King reached for the hem of her dress, his fingers toying with the fabric. "Let's get you out of this," he said before pausing to see what her reaction would be.

Ella let out a shaky breath as she nodded.

And with that, he began to undress her without rushing and with care. His every touch sent a spark of arousal all the way down to her core. Her panties were already drenched, and there was a ball of tension between her legs that she'd never felt before. Maybe she was being dramatic, but it felt as if it wasn't released, she would die.

King lifted Ella with ease, his strong hands gripping her thighs as he encouraged her to lay down. She let out a small gasp as her back met the soft mattress, her heart beating wildly. He hovered over her, his dark eyes scanning her face for a second before he pressed a kiss to her collarbone and then moved lower.

"You're so beautiful, baby," he murmured right before he latched onto one of her nipples.

The sensation made her jerk in surprise and stare down at him as he sucked her sensitive peak.

"Who do you belong to, baby?" he asked as he moved to the other side.

Ella shuddered at the possessiveness in his tone, her fingers clutching at his shoulders. "You, Daddy. I belong to you."

He hummed his approval and pulled away from her breast. "That's right, dollface. You belong to me. I'm going to take care of you."

"Breathe, baby," he whispered, his hands sliding down her sides. "Just let me take care of you."

Ella exhaled shakily, her body arching into his touch as he kissed, licked, and nipped at her. When she reached for his shirt, he quickly helped her pull it off and then returned to worshipping her body while she used her hands to explore his muscular, tattooed torso.

She'd felt King's cock through his pants before, so she knew it was large, but as she tried to unbuckle his belt, her fingers trembled. He wouldn't hurt her. She knew that, but she was still nervous. The only time she'd had sex had been so uncomfortable.

As if he could read her mind, he paused and reached for his jeans, and finished stripping off his clothes. When he pulled his underwear down and let his dick spring free, she gasped and stared at it with wide eyes.

"Relax, baby. I'm going to make you nice and ready for me," he reassured.

He moved over her again and lowered himself so his face was near her pussy. When he looked up at her and pressed a kiss above her hood, she melted. She wasn't sure how a man as tough as King could be so tender, but somehow, for her, he was.

"Spread your legs nice and wide for me, dollface. Let me see your pretty pussy."

A whimper escaped as she obeyed, the cool air brushing against her damp skin. King licked his lips and stared at her with hunger. Then he lowered his mouth to her clit, and she nearly burst into a million pieces. Everything around her went fuzzy, and all she could do was feel the pressure building higher and higher.

"Daddy," she cried out. "Oh, God."

He used his tongue and teeth to tease her clit while he brought a finger to her opening and slowly pressed in.

"That's my good girl. So sweet, so beautiful," he praised

gently. "Touch your breasts, baby. Show me how you touch them."

Heat spread over her, but she did as she was told and cupped her aching globes, kneading them gently before running her fingertips over the nipples. A moan escaped her lips, and he groaned against her clit, sending a vibration of pleasure through her.

Every touch, lick, kiss, and bite sent shockwaves through her, building her arousal until it was almost painful in the best way possible. Then he added another digit to her pussy, stretching her around his fingers and curling them to brush against that secret spot inside.

Ella screamed and shrieked, slapping the bed as she came apart. It was almost too much, but not enough at the same time. She wanted more. She wanted him.

"Daddy, please fuck me," she whined. "I need you."

King didn't move, didn't stop. He kept licking and sucking as he thrust his fingers in and out of her, her climax going higher and higher the more he did.

When she stopped shaking, he finally gave her what she wanted and crawled up her body, the head of his cock hovering at her entrance. He reached over to the nightstand, and a second later, she heard foil ripping, and then he started nudging inside of her.

"Hold on to me, baby. Tell me to stop if it hurts," he told her, his eyes searching hers.

She gripped his shoulders, wiggling her hips to adjust to the intrusion as he slowly pushed into her. He was thick but took his time, gritting his teeth the entire time. Ella almost felt bad that he was struggling so much, but she knew he wouldn't want it any other way. King would always put his comfort second to hers, which was one of the many reasons he was such an amazing Daddy.

"Fuck, baby. Are you okay?" he asked.

Nodding, she hooked her ankles behind his ass and pulled

him in more, the sensation sending a shiver through her as she stretched around him.

When his hips finally met hers, he paused and leaned down to kiss her. They both got lost in it and soon, they moved together in rhythm with their mouths. It started slowly, making love to each other in a way that felt incredibly intimate. Like their souls were talking to one another.

By the time their mouths parted, their movements were more desperate. Harder, deeper, longer. Ella cried out, her eyes locked on his while he fucked her. Her arousal coated his cock, making it more pleasurable for both of them.

King reached between them and pressed his thumb to her clit, stroking it with each thrust until she was screaming out again, her entire body quivering under him. He pumped harder and faster, then his movements became more erratic and wild until he came with her, his cock pulsing inside her.

When her cries quieted, and his movements slowed, a slow, lazy grin fell over her lips as her eyes closed, and she floated on the high of the most beautiful moment she'd ever experienced.

TWENTY
KING

King lay beside Ella, his large hand gently tracing up and down her back, feeling the slow, steady rise and fall of her breaths. She was curled against him, wrapped up in his warmth, her body completely relaxed in his arms. The glow from the bedside lamp cast soft shadows over her delicate features. Her cheeks were still flushed, and her lips were slightly parted in contentment.

His chest ached at the sight of her. She looked so small in his arms, so utterly vulnerable, and something deep inside him clenched tightly.

Mine. Forever.

He carefully kissed her forehead before sliding out of the bed. Ella whimpered at the loss of him, her fingers twitching as if searching for him.

"I'm right here, baby," he told her, brushing his knuckles over her cheek. "Just gonna get you cleaned up."

She hummed sleepily, barely opening her eyes and giving him a small nod.

King retrieved a warm, wet washcloth and gently wiped her skin, his touch careful. He wanted Ella to feel incredibly loved and taken care of. When he was done, he pulled the blankets up around her, tucking them in securely around her before pressing another soft kiss to her temple.

"I'll be right back, Little one," he whispered.

Ella made a sleepy sound of protest but didn't stop him as he slipped out of the room. In the kitchen, he grabbed a bottle of water and a bar of chocolate he had stashed away.

When he returned, Ella had shifted onto her side, her eyes opening slightly as she peeked up at him. So fucking sweet and adorable. Perfect.

King sat on the edge of the bed, brushing her hair back before offering her the water. "Drink, baby."

She obeyed, taking slow sips before handing the bottle back. He smiled, pleased, then unwrapped the chocolate and held it up to her lips. "A little something sweet for my sweet girl."

Ella giggled softly and took a bite. "You're spoiling me."

"Damn right, I am." King tucked the blankets even closer around her. "You deserve it."

When she finished, he slid back into bed, pulling her against his chest. He wrapped his arms around her, slipping one hand beneath the covers to rest against the warm skin of her lower back. Ella let out a small, content sigh.

He pressed his lips to her hair, inhaling deeply. "You did so good for me, baby," he whispered. "I'm so proud of you."

Ella let out a sleepy hum, her fingers tracing his chest lazily. "Thanks, Daddy. You didn't do so bad yourself."

King laughed and shook his head. His silly girl. "Glad to hear it, dollface. Maybe I'll give you a comment card so I can do even better next time."

She grinned and waggled her eyebrows. "That's a great idea. I look forward to filling it out."

He stared down at her with a permanent smile as her breathing slowed, and soon, she was completely asleep in his arms. King continued to lay awake, his heart racing.

He was in love with Ella.

Completely and utterly in love.

And it was the best feeling he'd ever experienced.

King sat at one of the tables in the clubhouse, eating a sandwich while a few of the Littles giggled and chatted a few seats away. He wasn't paying much attention until he caught his name in the mix of their conversation.

"We should tell King," Carlee said, nudging Ivy.

"Tell me what?" King asked, glancing up from his plate, his brows raising slightly.

What kind of trouble were the brats getting into, and why did they want to drag him into it?

Ivy grinned, twisting her juice box between her hands. "We were talking about the food drive. There's still so much stuff that needs to be collected, right?"

King set his sandwich on his plate. "Yeah, the need is way higher than anyone expected."

"Well," Remi piped up, leaning forward with excitement, "since the MC has such a big presence in town, why don't we throw a big party? Like a charity event. We can invite everyone in Shadowridge and get them to bring donations for the food drive."

King sat back, rubbing his jaw as he thought about it. It was a damn good idea. Maybe he shouldn't have assumed the Littles were up to no good.

The club had hosted events before, and they always drew a crowd. If they turned it into a full-on party with food, music, and games, they could bring in a lot of extra supplies for families in need.

"That's actually brilliant," he admitted, flashing the girls a grin. "I'll talk to Steele and Storm about it."

The Littles cheered, high-fiving each other as King pushed up from the table and made his way to find the men.

When he explained the idea, both of them were on board immediately.

"Yeah, we can hold it here at the compound," Storm agreed, crossing his arms. "Plenty of space, and people love partying with the MC. If we market it as a charity event, they'll be even more likely to show up."

"I'll call a few vendors," Steele added. "See if we can get some food trucks or something. Maybe a band, too."

King nodded, already feeling the excitement building. "I'll run it by Ella. I know she's been stressed about getting enough donations. This could make a huge difference."

Minutes later, King was on his Harley, riding through town toward City Hall. The wind whipped against him as he rode, but something felt off.

As he weaved through the streets of Shadowridge, he couldn't shake the idea that someone was following him.

He checked his mirrors.

Nothing.

A few cars were behind him, the usual afternoon, but no one familiar. No one that stood out.

Still, the feeling lingered. Normally, it wouldn't bother him, but they'd been having issues with another MC lately, and he didn't fully trust that the Devil's Jesters were done being a problem.

By the time he pulled up to City Hall, he was on edge. He parked his bike and shook the feeling off, telling himself he was being paranoid. His focus needed to be on Ella.

Inside, he found her at her desk, looking adorable as ever, her head bent over a stack of papers. When she looked up and saw him, her face lit up.

"Hey, Daddy," she said softly, a little smile curling her lips.

His chest warmed as he leaned down to press a kiss to her temple.

"Hey, dollface," he murmured, stepping closer. "Got a minute?"

She set her pen down. "Always."

King rested against her desk, explaining the idea the Littles had come up with. As he spoke, Ella's excitement grew, her eyes sparkling.

"That's such a good idea!" she gasped. "This could be exactly what we need to fill the gaps. But... Are you sure the MC wants to go through all that trouble? This is supposed to be my project to manage."

He reached out and cupped her chin. "You're part of the MC. And the MC is part of this community. We care about the people here, so if we can do something to make Shadowridge a better place for families, we'll be on board."

Tears filled her eyes as she beamed at him. "What can I do to help?"

King smiled, pleased by her genuine reaction. "We'll start planning tonight. We'll go over logistics, make a list of what we need, and get the word out fast. Steele has already reached out to some vendors. Don't worry, baby. We've got this. As a team."

Ella wiggled in her seat. "Maybe I can talk to Mayor Winslow about promoting it, too."

"Good thinking," King said, brushing a strand of hair behind her ear.

She grinned at him. In that moment, he was reminded again how much he loved this woman.

"I'll let you get back to work. I'm gonna head back to the clubhouse. It's supposed to start raining in a few hours, and I don't want to be riding when it starts."

"Okay." Ella stood and walked around her desk, then threw her arms around his waist. "Thank you, Daddy. You're the best ever."

"Anything for you, Little girl."

He kissed the top of her head one last time and headed back outside, only to stop short when he reached his bike.

His front tire was flat.

King's eyes narrowed as he crouched down to inspect it. A slow, uneasy realization crept through him as he inspected the obvious slice in the rubber.

Someone had done this.

Jaw tightening, he pulled out his phone and dialed Kade.

"Brother," Kade answered. "What's up?"

"Need a tow and a ride," King muttered, scanning the street around him. "Someone's slashed my tire."

There was a pause, then a sharp exhale. "You sure?"

"Yeah," King confirmed, standing up, his shoulders tensing. "And I think I was being followed earlier."

"Stay put. I'm on my way."

Just as King hung up, the sky opened up, and rain poured down in huge, heavy drops.

King let out a low, humorless chuckle, shaking his head. "Figures. Fuck."

TWENTY-ONE
ELLA

Ella smoothed out her skirt, clutching her notepad as she knocked on Mayor Winslow's office door.

"Come in," the mayor's familiar voice called out.

Ella stepped inside, offering him a warm smile as she approached. He looked up from his paperwork, his sharp but kind eyes meeting hers. "Ah, Ella. What can I do for you?"

She took a seat in front of his desk and set her notepad on her lap. Working for Mayor Winslow had been wonderful so far. He was as kind as he seemed, and he truly cared about the citizens of Shadowridge. He also gave her a lot of freedom, telling her he trusted that she was fully competent to do the job in her own way. It was nice to work for someone so down to earth.

"I wanted to run an idea by you—something that could help bring in more donations for the food drive and possibly even donations to get an early start on the summer drive for school supplies."

The mayor leaned back in his chair, folding his hands in front of him. "I'm listening."

Ella took a breath, excitement bubbling in her chest. "The Shadowridge Guardians have offered to throw a charity event at their compound. Kind of like a town party. They'll invite everyone, have food, games, music, and make the entrance fee a food, coat, backpack, or a cash donation."

Mayor Winslow's brows lifted, intrigued.

"King thought it would be a great way to bring the community together while also increasing donations," she continued. "The MC has a strong presence in town, and I think people would show up in huge numbers. It would be totally family-friendly."

The mayor nodded slowly, considering. After a moment, a wide smile spread across his face. "That," he smiled, "is an excellent idea."

Ella beamed. "Really?"

He let out a chuckle. "Absolutely. The Guardians may have a rough exterior, but they've always been good for Shadowridge. If they're willing to host the party, I say we make this happen." He tapped a pen against his desk. "You've done a fantastic job, Ella. Honestly, I don't know how I ever survived without you. Besides the food drive, you've been managing a million other things with such ease."

Ella's chest warmed at the praise. "Thank you, sir. I just... really want to help, and I've fallen in love with this town already."

Mayor Winslow studied her for a long moment before leaning forward. "When I first hired you, I wasn't sure how someone from your upbringing would fit in here."

Ella's heart stuttered. She knew what he meant. A lot of people from the social circles she came from knew nothing about charity or need, nor did they care. Unless it was to show up at a huge fundraiser in expensive couture and act like they wanted to help, they weren't interested. It was one of the reasons why she'd never understood why her parents stayed around those people. Her mom and dad were different. They did care about others, and they didn't make a big show for other people to know. Sometimes, she wondered if they would like it here in Shadowridge. But living somewhere different had been her dream. As long as they were happy, that's all that mattered to her.

He gave her a small smile. "But you've proved me wrong. You care. Not just about the work but about the people. And that's exactly the kind of person we need in this office."

Ella swallowed hard, emotion tightening in her throat.

"That being said," he continued, "I know you're still within your ninety-day probation period, but I'd like to hire you permanently. Effective immediately. With a raise."

Her mouth fell open. "I—what?"

He chuckled. "You've earned it, Ella. You work hard, and you care. That's what matters."

Tears welled in her eyes. "Thank you," she whispered, barely able to believe what she was hearing.

"It might be too soon for you to know if you're staying permanently here, but the offer is on the table."

Ella wiped at her eyes, laughing softly. "I'd love to stay. I've already decided I never want to leave Shadowridge."

The next several days blurred into one. Ella spent her mornings at City Hall, working on the logistics of the charity party. By the afternoons, she bounced between meetings with vendors, coordinated flyers and social media announcements, and checked in with King and the Guardians MC about the event setup.

And every night, she ended up in King's arms.

Each evening when she arrived at the clubhouse, King was already waiting for her, sometimes leaning against his Harley, sometimes inside the common area, always watching her with that adoration that made her heart race. The moment she stepped into his space, he was there, taking her bag from her shoulder, guiding her inside, pressing a lingering kiss to her forehead before asking, "What have you eaten today, Little one?"

Every night, he took care of her. He made sure she ate a proper meal, even when she pouted because he wouldn't let her survive on candy salad. He bathed her, washing her hair with strong, careful fingers, then sat by the edge while she played with bath toys that he'd bought her. He tucked her into his bed, settled in beside her, and wrapped her up in his arms as if he were afraid she might disappear if he didn't hold on tightly enough.

It was almost effortless between them. They fit together and were exactly what each other needed.

And it wasn't just him.

Whenever she had free time, she hung out with the other Littles, who she already considered her best friends.

They played hide-and-seek around the compound, giggled over coloring books and craft projects, and cuddled up together during movie nights in the common room. The clubhouse was filled with warmth, laughter, and love, and for the first time in her life, Ella didn't feel like an outsider looking in.

She *belonged*.

Sometimes, she missed her parents. She still called them every few days. They always asked how she was doing, always reminded her that she could come home anytime. But every time she ended the call, she looked around at the life she had started in Shadowridge, the one she was building with King, and she knew.

She *was* home.

And as she stood in the clubhouse one night, watching King go over the final party details with Steele and Storm, she felt it deep in her bones.

Life couldn't possibly get any better than this.

TWENTY-TWO
KING

King leaned against the counter of the small kitchenette in his apartment, arms crossed, watching Ella, who was hunched over her laptop at the small table in the corner. The soft glow from the screen flickered across her face, highlighting the determined furrow of her brow as her fingers danced over the keyboard.

He sighed and glanced at the clock. "All right, Little one," he said, his voice steady but firm. "It's time for bed."

Ella barely spared him a glance. "I'll go in a little while," she mumbled, still focused on her screen. "I just have to finish this first."

King's jaw ticked as he stepped forward. "Baby, it's already thirty minutes past your bedtime. You can finish that tomorrow."

"I know," she said sweetly, though she still didn't look up from her laptop. "Just a few more minutes, Daddy."

King narrowed his eyes slightly. She was testing him.

"Ella." His voice dropped lower, laced with warning.

She finally glanced up, wide-eyed and innocent, blinking as if she had no idea what he was about to do. "What?"

King tilted his head, his tone firm but calm. "I said it's time for bed. That wasn't a suggestion."

For a moment, guilt flickered in her eyes, but instead of closing her laptop, she turned back to the screen and typed faster. "Just a few more minutes," she insisted.

King let out a slow exhale, his patience thinning. "All right, baby. Have it your way."

In three long strides, he was at the table. Before Ella realized what was happening, he reached down and plucked her right out of her chair.

"Daddy!" she squealed, her laptop snapping shut as she kicked her feet. "I wasn't done."

King ignored her struggles, adjusting his grip as she wiggled wildly in his arms. "You're done for the night, Little girl," he said evenly. "And since you didn't listen the first time, I think you need a reminder about what happens when you ignore Daddy."

Ella gasped, realization dawning in her eyes. "Nooo, Daddy, wait! I didn't—"

"Oh, you did," King interrupted as he walked them both toward the bed. "You knew *exactly* what you were doing."

She squirmed harder, whining in protest, but he was stronger. He sat on the edge of the bed and effortlessly adjusted her so that she was face-down over his lap, her bottom perfectly positioned for what was coming.

Ella whimpered, her body tensing.

"I just wanted to finish my work," she pouted.

"And I just wanted you in bed on time. You've been working a lot of hours this week and staying up late, and I've been allowing it because I know how important this is to you. But, as your Daddy, it's my job to take care of you and draw the line when it's affecting your health or happiness. You're not going to be able to do either of those things if you're so exhausted you can't function," King countered, rubbing his large palm over the curve of her backside. "Your job as my Little girl is to obey me, which you chose not to do. And now, you're going to learn why that was a mistake."

He lifted his hand and brought it down with a loud smack over her thin leggings. Then he did it to the other cheek, and almost immediately, she started wiggling.

"I'm sorry, Daddy."

It was much too late for that. His girl was going to learn a lesson, and then he was going to tuck her into bed where she belonged.

"You're not sorry yet, but you will be when I'm done."

Over and over, he spanked her, alternating cheeks. She whimpered and apologized with almost every swat. The last thing he ever wanted to do was hurt his girl, but this was part of their dynamic. And King suspected that she needed this spanking more than she realized.

He was so proud of her for all the hard work she'd been doing, but she was spreading herself too thinly, and he wouldn't continue to allow that. The fundraiser wasn't worth harming her health. In fact, he probably should have had Doc give Ella an exam as a precaution. He would have to talk to his friend about that tomorrow.

When he could feel the heat of her bottom through her leggings and panties, he tucked his hand in the waistband of both and pulled them down together. Ella let out a cry of protest and tried to reach back to stop him, but he was too quick. He grabbed hold of her wrist and pinned it to her lower back, then started spanking her once again, peppering her entire bottom.

"I love you, Little girl. It's my job to take care of you, and I take that responsibility very seriously."

Her cries stopped, and she twisted to look back at him with watery eyes. "You love me?"

Pausing, he pinned her with a stare. "Yes, baby girl. More than anything. I'm so fucking in love with you it's not even funny. You're mine, and I take care of what's mine, even if your bottom pays the price."

She let out a sob as tears spilled down her cheeks. "I love you too, Daddy."

It was as if a dam had broken, and all the emotions she'd been bottling up for however long came pouring out of her. He started spanking her again, wanting her to get it all out. When she finally went limp over his lap, he stopped and pulled her into his arms to comfort her while she cried her eyes out against his chest.

He sat quietly, rocking her against him for several minutes until her sobs became whimpers and then the occasional hiccup.

"That's my good girl. Let's get you ready for bed, yeah? Then I'll snuggle you all night long."

She nodded but stayed silent, and when he held up the pacifier to her, she immediately opened her lips and started suckling on it. He worked quickly to get her changed into a nightie and pair of training panties and then carried her into the bathroom to use the toilet. The entire time, she was fighting to stay awake. She was truly his Little girl right then, letting him take control and take care of her.

After she went potty, he cleaned her up and washed his hands, then carried her back to the bed, where he tucked her in next to her stuffed rabbit.

"Thirsty," she murmured.

Smiling, he went to the kitchenette and filled one of the baby bottles he'd grabbed from the closet with water. This was the first time he'd given her a bottle, and just as he expected, as soon as he held the nipple to her lips, she opened her mouth and sucked down the cold liquid.

"My sweet baby. Just sleep, dollface. Daddy's got you," he whispered.

She let out a contented sigh, and within seconds, her breathing turned shallow, and she was out for the night.

King wiped a bead of sweat from his forehead, stepping back to survey the clubhouse's main lot. The place was buzzing as the final touches came together. His MC brothers worked like a well-oiled machine—setting up tables, stringing up lights, and ensuring that everything was in place for the fundraising party.

It was chaotic, but it worked for all of them. With so many Littles around, they were used to chaos.

Across the lot, the Littles were hard at work decorating, their giggles carrying over the noise of last-minute preparations. Carlee and Ivy were blowing up balloons—though half of them ended up getting batted around like playthings—while Remi and Harper tied colorful streamers to every available surface. Ella stood in the center of it all, directing everyone with a nervous energy that King could see from a mile away.

She had been worrying non-stop about it all, and even though he knew it would be a success, he understood how important this was for her.

With a shake of his head, he turned back to Steele and Atlas, who were hauling in crates of food and drinks.

"We good on the catering setup?" King asked, lifting a hand to adjust the collar of his cut.

It was the perfect day for this. Warm and sunny with a gentle breeze in the air.

Steele nodded. "Yeah, food trucks are parking along the right-hand side of the clubhouse. Bartender's setting up inside for the adults, and we've got plenty of non-alcoholic stuff for the kids and Littles."

"Games?"

Storm walked past, giving King a thumbs-up. "Bouncy house is good to go, dunk tank's filling up, and Doc's got the face-painting table sorted."

King grinned. *Perfect.* Everything was coming together as he'd hoped, but there was still one thing left—his surprise for Ella. But that would come after the party started.

He spotted her standing near the entrance of the compound, nervously chewing on her lip. He took a second to watch her, admiring how she threw herself into the event planning. It was important to her, which was one of the many reasons he loved her so much. She cared about others, and it showed.

She looked beautiful—hair pinned back with a small bow, wearing a sundress that flowed down to her knees, and a pair of sparkly sandals that matched her personality perfectly.

My girl.

King made his way over, stepping behind her and wrapping his arms around her waist. She jumped slightly, but when she realized who it was, she immediately relaxed against him.

"Daddy," she sighed, resting her head on his chest. "I feel like I'm forgetting something."

"You're not," he murmured, pressing a kiss to the top of her head. "You've done an amazing job, Little one. This is going to be perfect."

She turned in his arms, looking up at him with big, worried eyes. "What if no one shows up?"

King snorted. "Baby, the whole damn town is buzzing about this party. I'm pretty sure we're going to have more people than we expect."

Ella exhaled, some of the tension leaving her shoulders. "You really think it's going to go well?"

King cupped her cheek, rubbing his thumb against her soft skin. "I *know* it is. And I couldn't be prouder of you, baby."

Her eyes shimmered, and a slow smile spread across her lips. "You mean that?"

King chuckled, shaking his head. "Damn right, I do. Look at everything you've done, Ella. You put this together, you worked your ass off for it, and now the whole town's coming out because *you* care enough to make sure these families get what they need." He tipped her chin up slightly, staring down at her. "I couldn't be prouder to call you mine."

Ella's breath hitched, her fingers clutching at the front of his cut.

"There's something else I wanna ask you," he said, letting his hand trail down to her waist.

Ella blinked. "What, Daddy?"

King exhaled, his gaze steady. "Move in with me, baby. Permanently."

For a split second, Ella stared at him like she couldn't process the words. Then, suddenly, she gasped loudly before launching herself into his arms with so much force that he had to take a step back to keep his balance.

"Yes!" she squealed, her legs wrapping around his waist.

King let out a deep laugh, catching her with ease as she peppered kisses all over his face.

"Well, damn," he teased. "Didn't think you'd be that excited."

Ella pulled back, grinning ear to ear. "Are you kidding? Of course I'm excited. I want to be with you every day, Daddy. I mean, I've pretty much been living with you anyway."

It was true. He had only taken her home every couple of days to grab more clothes or whatever she needed, but she hadn't slept at her place since they'd become official.

He chuckled, brushing his nose against hers. "Then it's settled, Little one."

She sighed happily, nuzzling against his neck. "I love you, Daddy."

King held her tightly, breathing her in, knowing without a doubt that he had everything he'd ever wanted right there in his arms. "I love you, too, dollface. Now, take a breath, and let's get this party started, yeah?"

TWENTY-THREE
ELLA

Ella practically bounced across the compound, barely able to contain the excitement bubbling inside her. She had to tell someone. The news was practically exploding from her.

She spotted Remi, Harper, Carlee, Ivy, Molly, and the rest of the Littles gathered near the dessert table, setting out trays of cookies and cupcakes, chatting animatedly as they worked.

"I have big news," Ella practically shouted as she skidded to a stop in front of them.

The girls turned to her in surprise before their eyes widened in anticipation.

"What? What is it?" Remi shrieked, immediately grabbing her hands.

Ella grinned so hard her cheeks ached. "I'm moving in with King."

A split second of silence—then *chaos*.

The Littles screamed excitedly, jumping up and down, clapping their hands, and bombarding her with hugs.

"Oh my gosh!" Harper practically tackled her in a hug. "You get to live here now? Like, for real? We'll be able to hang out and have slumber parties when our Daddies are on shift!"

Ella giggled, hugging her back. "Oh my gosh, it's going to be so fun."

"This is the best news ever," Ivy beamed. "We were hoping you'd stay forever."

Ella laughed, overwhelmed by all their love and enthusiasm. She couldn't believe how much her life had changed—how quickly she had found not only a Daddy who adored her, but a group of best friends who made every day feel brighter, too.

"I love you guys," she gushed, squeezing them all again before stepping back. "But I have to get back to work. The party's starting soon, and there's still so much to do."

The girls all hurried back to their tasks.

As Ella double-checked the sign-in table, making sure the donation bins were properly labeled, she noticed King talking to an older couple near the clubhouse entrance.

Her heart skipped. His parents. He had mentioned they might come, but she'd been so busy planning that she hadn't thought much about it. Shoot. What if they didn't like her?

Before she could fully worry about it, King turned and motioned for her to come over.

She took a deep breath, smoothed out her sundress, and forced herself to walk over at a normal pace, even though her limbs suddenly felt tangled.

"Mom, Dad," King introduced as she reached them, his hand settling possessively on her lower back. "This is Ella."

His mother, a beautiful woman with soft eyes and a kind smile, immediately reached out and pulled Ella into a hug. "Oh, sweetheart," she said warmly, holding her tightly. "It is so good to meet you."

Ella blinked in surprise before melting into her embrace. "It's so nice to meet you, too."

When King's mother pulled back, his father stepped forward, giving Ella a firm but gentle handshake. "King's told us a lot about you," he said kindly. "We're glad to see him so happy."

Ella felt a wave of warmth rush over her.

"He makes me really happy, too," she admitted shyly, glancing up at King.

His mother beamed, squeezing her hands. "We're thrilled you're moving in with him. That boy has never looked at anyone the way he looks at you. I can already tell you two were made for each other."

Ella blushed furiously. "I feel really lucky."

King squeezed her waist and pressed a kiss to her temple. "We both are, baby."

The moment was so sweet and perfect until a small ache settled in her chest.

Her parents weren't there.

She loved King's family already, and their kindness made her feel so incredibly welcome, but she couldn't help the small pang of sadness that her own mom and dad weren't here to meet King, to see her success, and to see the life she was building in Shadowridge.

She wondered what they would think of all this. Of him. She suspected her mother would blush at how handsome he was.

Before she could get lost in those thoughts, a commotion from the parking lot caught her attention.

She turned, and her breath hitched.

A long line of cars was steadily pulling into the lot, people stepping out with bags and boxes of food. Some carried stacks of canned goods, while others rolled in carts packed with dry goods and supplies. Families, couples, local business owners—so many people were here, all eager to help.

Ella felt her sadness dissolve as pure joy took over.

"They came," she whispered, almost disbelieving.

King chuckled beside her. "Told you, baby. This was all you."

Ella turned to him, eyes shining. *"We* did this."

He grinned and winked at her. "Damn right we did."

The party was more than Ella ever could have imagined.

People filled the compound, mingling beneath the twinkling lights strung across the lot. The air was filled with laughter, playing, music, and the comforting hum of community spirit. The food trucks were a hit, their delicious aromas mixing with the scent of barbecue from the grill station, where Steele and Doc flipped burgers like they were competing for a championship title.

But it wasn't the turnout that had Ella feeling like she was floating—it was the sheer amount of donations.

Everywhere she looked, there were bins overflowing with canned goods, boxes of pasta, baby supplies, hygiene products, and so much more. Every table was stacked high with bags of food, and volunteers from the food bank were busy sorting everything, their smiles wide and their voices full of excitement.

They had crushed their goal and then some.

Ella stood near the welcome table, staring in awe at everything, her heart swelling so much she thought it might burst.

"I can't believe this," she whispered, shaking her head in disbelief.

King's warm arm wrapped around her waist, snuggling her against his side. "Believe it, dollface. This is what small-town living is all about. Community."

Ella turned, looking up at him, her eyes shining.

King cupped her face in his warm hands. "Be proud, Little one. You've done an amazing job here."

She was.

She was so unbelievably proud.

And happy.

The entire time, King stayed by her side, his presence steady and reassuring. He made sure she was drinking water, bringing her small bites of real food between conversations so she wouldn't get distracted and forget to eat. Everyone at the party wanted to talk to her, even briefly, to tell her what a great success it had been and that they hoped it would happen again. Ella was more than overwhelmed, and her heart was so full that it was impossible not to smile all night.

"Three bites, baby," King instructed as he held up a plate in between her chatting with guests.

"But—"

"No buts. Eat."

She giggled and obeyed, unable to deny how much she loved that he took care of her, even in his own bossy way.

And truly, she couldn't imagine a more perfect night.

Until she heard them.

A familiar voice behind her—warm and loving.

"Darling!"

Ella froze.

Slowly, she turned around.

And there they were.

Her parents.

Standing a few feet away, watching her with equal parts pride and overwhelming emotion.

Ella's hands flew to her mouth. "Mom? Dad?"

Tears welled in her mother's eyes as she smiled. "Ella," she whispered, already stepping forward.

Ella launched herself into their arms, tears spilling down her cheeks before she could stop them. "You're here," she gasped, clinging to them as they wrapped her up in a tight hug.

Her father chuckled. "Of course we are, kiddo."

Ella pulled back just enough to look at them, still in complete shock. "But... how? When? Why didn't you tell me?"

Her mother cupped her cheek, smiling softly. "We wanted to surprise you. King called us."

Ella blinked. "King?"

Her father nodded, glancing past her. "He said you'd been working so hard on this and that he knew how much you were missing us. He wanted us to see what an incredible job you've done here."

Ella's chest ached with emotion.

She turned slowly, her gaze finding him.

King stood a few feet away, arms crossed over his broad chest, watching the reunion unfold with a small, satisfied smirk.

Ella raced toward him, throwing herself into his arms.

He caught her with ease, letting out a low chuckle as he wrapped her in his arms tightly. "Hi, Little one."

Ella buried her face against his neck. "You called them?"

"Figured you'd want them here."

She pulled back to cup his face, her eyes shimmering. "I love you. I can't believe you did this."

"I'd do anything for you, baby. I love you."

A second later, her parents approached them, and Ella made introductions. Just as she suspected, her mother's cheeks turned pink as she shook King's hand, and when the men weren't paying attention, her mom winked at Ella as if to say *good job.*

The four of them got lost in conversation quickly, her father asking King all about the MC and his motorcycle. When her dad mentioned possibly getting a Harley of his own, Ella nearly spewed her water all over him.

"Dad? A motorcycle? Really?" Ella asked.

Her mother tilted her head and smiled. "I don't know. I think your father would look pretty sexy on a bike."

King grinned as Ella's face flushed. Good Lord, she'd forgotten how gooey her parents were with each other. They were so cute together, though.

When her father asked to see King's bike and the two men

disappeared, her mother linked arms with her as they headed inside to get a drink.

"Darling, that man is head over heels in love with you. Don't ever let him go, or I might have to leave your father and snatch him up myself. I could be one of those panthers or whatever you call them."

Ella burst out laughing. "A cougar, Mom?"

Her mother giggled. "Yes, one of those."

"Well, unfortunately for you, I'm never letting King go."

"Well, pooey. I guess I'll have to get your dad one of those leather cut things that King's wearing, and we'll have to role-play then."

Oh, dear God. She loved her parents.

"I'll see what I can do about getting Dad a cut… But only if you promise never to mention role-playing with my father ever again."

Her mom huffed out a laugh. "Deal."

TWENTY-FOUR
KING

The bonfire burned bright against the dark, starlit sky. Laughter and conversation filled the air, music still playing from the speakers near the clubhouse. The night had been perfect. Better than King could've ever hoped.

He stood outside the main building, a bottle of water in one hand as he chatted with Ella's parents. To his relief, they seemed to genuinely like him. More than that, they seemed to *approve* of him, which was a huge fucking win. He had worried they might not agree with his tattoos or lifestyle, but it seemed the opposite. They were truly down to earth, which wasn't what he'd expected. It was a pleasant surprise.

"We're so happy we made the trip." Ella's mother smiled warmly at him. "It's obvious how much she loves it here. And how much you love her."

King's chest swelled at her words, and he nodded, rubbing the back of his neck. "She's my whole world," he admitted, glancing toward the garden where many of the Littles were still giggling and playing near the swing set. "I'd do anything for her."

Ella's father studied him for a long moment, then gave a slow nod of approval. "That's what we like to hear."

King smiled softly. "You don't have to worry about her with me. She's got me wrapped around her finger."

Her parents chuckled, and then her mother casually added, "We were talking about something on the way here. We arrived yesterday and have been touring Shadowridge."

King tilted his head. "Yeah?"

Ella's father smiled. "We love it here. It's charming, small but lively, and most importantly, it's where Ella is." He exchanged a glance with his wife before continuing, "We've been thinking about getting a second home here. Something small, so we can visit her as much as possible."

King felt a surge of warmth spread through him. "That'd be incredible," he said sincerely. "She misses you guys a lot. Having you close, even part-time, would mean everything to her."

Ella's mother smiled. "That's what we were thinking, too. We hope you know we never meant to hurt Ella by staying in New York. All we've ever wanted is what's best for her. We were born as only children into the biggest real-estate families in the state, and we were expected to continue the businesses. Our marriage was a business deal. We were just lucky that we truly fell in love." The older couple smiled softly at each other before she continued. "Anyway, we always wished for Ella to live the life she wanted. We were so proud of her when she told us she wanted to start her own life. All we've ever wanted to do was support her. We tried to protect her from the harshness of our society, but I don't think we did a very good job."

King shook his head and offered a reassuring smile. "I think you guys did an amazing job. Ella is the most amazing woman I've ever met. She's compassionate, bubbly, full of life, and she has told me what great parents you are."

It seemed as if his words soothed their worry because her mom gave his arm a gentle squeeze.

His eyes flicked toward the clubhouse. It had been a while since Ella had excused herself to the bathroom. He assumed she got caught up talking to someone. She had a habit of getting distracted, and it seemed like everyone wanted to talk to her tonight, but still… it had been too long.

A small prickle of unease crawled up his spine.

"Excuse me for a second," he said to Ella's parents, glancing toward the clubhouse. "Just gonna check on her."

He made his way through the lingering guests.

When he ran into a few of the Littles, he stopped to ask them. "Anyone seen Ella?"

"Nope," Ivy answered, shaking her head. "Did she go inside?"

"Said she was going to the bathroom."

Remi frowned. "That was a while ago, wasn't it?"

King's jaw tensed. "Yeah."

Pulling out his phone, he called her.

No answer.

His gut twisted as he went into the clubhouse. He went to the common area restroom first and knocked. "Baby?" he called.

No response.

He checked inside quickly, but it was empty.

His pulse kicked up.

Where the hell did she go?

After checking his apartment bathroom, he walked outside again, scanning the compound. The bonfire cast long shadows across the lot, but he didn't see her anywhere. The Littles were still gathered together, but she wasn't with them.

His unease deepened.

He tried her phone again.

No answer.

Something was wrong.

King turned, spotting Steele and Doc standing near the entrance. He strode toward them, his heart beginning to pound harder.

"You guys seen Ella?" he asked quickly.

Steele shook his head, immediately on alert from King's tone. "Not for a bit. Why?"

"She went to the bathroom and never returned," King said tightly. "She's not answering her phone, but I don't know whether she had it on her or not."

Atlas and Kade walked up, concern etched on their faces.

"Remi said you can't find Ella?" Kade asked.

"You think something's happened?" Doc asked, his sharp eyes narrowing.

King exhaled harshly, his chest tightening. "I don't know," he admitted, "but I don't like this. It's not like her to disappear. I need eyes everywhere. Now."

His brothers didn't hesitate.

"I'll search the clubhouse," Kade offered.

"Perimeter," Atlas added, already heading toward the back of the compound.

"Parking lot," Steele called out, already heading in that direction.

"I'll take the Littles inside," Doc said, nodding toward the others.

King's hands clenched into fists, a deep, cold dread settling inside him.

He didn't know what was happening.

But his gut was screaming at him.

And for the first time in a long time, he was scared.

TWENTY-FIVE
ELLA

Ella hummed softly as she made her way down the long hallway, feeling light and happy after freshening up in the bathroom. With all the water King had been making her drink, she'd nearly peed herself as she'd rushed inside. He was her bossy Daddy. And she loved him for it.

The night had been perfect. Better than she could've ever dreamed. The fundraiser was a success, King had been by her side all night, and her parents had surprised her by showing up.

She couldn't wait to get back outside to him.

But as she reached the end of the hallway, a figure suddenly stepped out from one of the side rooms, blocking her path.

Ella froze.

The dim light from the hallway lamps illuminated the woman's face, and recognition hit Ella like a punch to the gut.

Janelle.

King's *ex*.

Her blood ran cold.

Why is that bitch here?

Janelle stood with her arms crossed, a smug snarl curling her blood-red lips. She looked just as she had the day Ella had first seen her in the firehouse. Gorgeous in a way that was sharp rather than soft, dressed in tight jeans and a low-cut top that screamed confidence.

But her eyes?

Her eyes were filled with meanness and hate.

Ella squared her shoulders, forcing her voice to stay steady. "What are you doing here?"

Janelle let out a low, evil chuckle. "What do you think?" she sneered. "I came to get King back."

Ella's stomach twisted, but she refused to let this woman intimidate her. "He doesn't want you," she stated firmly. "You need to leave."

Janelle's smile faded, her expression twisting into something dark and dangerous. "And you think you can stop me?" she spat.

Ella took a step forward, suddenly hyper-aware of how alone they were in this part of the clubhouse. Everyone was outside at the party—no one would hear her if anything happened.

"I am stopping you," Ella snapped. "King and I are together. He loves me. Not you. You need to move on."

Janelle's entire body tensed, her hands curling into fists. For a brief second, Ella thought she might just storm past her—

But then, without warning, Janelle lunged.

Ella barely had time to react before Janelle shoved her with all her weight, forcing her backward into a darkened doorway. The unexpected force sent her stumbling, and as she tried to catch herself, her ankle twisted at an unnatural angle.

Pain exploded up her leg.

She let out a cry, collapsing onto the floor, her hands scrambling against the cold concrete.

Janelle stood over her, her expression smug.

"Pathetic," she hissed.

Ella tried to push herself up, but the sharp, throbbing agony in her ankle made her gasp.

Janelle's foot suddenly shot out, kicking Ella.

"You bitch!" Ella shouted as she tried again to get up.

But it was too late.

Janelle slammed the door shut.

Ella's heart dropped into her stomach as she heard the unmistakable sound of a lock turning from the outside.

Dread surged through her.

She scrambled to her feet. The pain in her ankle nearly sent her crashing back down, but she wouldn't let that stop her because she needed to get out of there. Then she was going to find Janelle and kick her ass.

The room was pitch black. She wasn't even sure what kind of room it was. A storage closet or a cleaning closet?

Oh, God, what if there were spiders in there?

Ella's breathing came faster, fear crawling up her spine.

She reached down, her fingers patting the sides of her dress frantically.

Then she froze.

She didn't have her phone with her.

She'd left it on the table outside because her dress didn't have pockets.

Shit!

Her heartbeat thundered in her ears as she stumbled to the door, pounding on it with her fists.

"Help!" she screamed. "Somebody help me!"

But outside, the party was still raging. The music, the laughter—it drowned her cries out completely.

Ella swallowed hard, pressing her forehead against the door as true panic set in.

She was locked in. Alone. In the dark. Possibly with spiders and rats and God knew what else.

And no one knew where she was.

TWENTY-SIX
KING

King moved through the compound with a tight jaw and a racing pulse, doing his best to keep his worry under control.

They would find her.

It was entirely possible she was outside somewhere, having a moment to herself. At least, that's what he hoped she was doing.

The last thing he wanted to do was cause a scene and put everyone on edge, but every second that passed without finding Ella made his chest tighten. His gut was screaming at him that something was wrong.

He checked the playground first, scanning the swings and slides where the Littles often played. Nothing.

He moved to the old oak tree on the edge of the property, where she loved to sit and read. Empty.

The motorcycle shop. Nothing.

His grip tightened around his phone as he walked the entire perimeter of the compound.

Where the hell was she?

As he turned the corner near the back of the clubhouse, his frustration mounting, he collided with someone.

He barely budged, but the person let out a small oof, taking a step back.

King's hands clenched into fists when he saw who it was.

Janelle.

His entire body went rigid. His already thin patience snapped at the sight of her, looking smug as ever.

She smiled up at him, brushing a hand over her low-cut top. "King. Daddy. I hoped I'd find you alone."

King's lip curled in disgust. "Where is she?" he growled.

There was no doubt in his mind Janelle had something to do with Ella's disappearance.

Janelle blinked innocently. "Who?"

His hands itched to grab her, to shake the truth out of her, but he forced himself to stay still. Barely.

"Don't play games with me, Janelle," he barked. "Where's Ella?"

She scoffed, rolling her eyes. "Why do you care? You had me once, and now you're wasting your time on *her*?" She took a step closer, lifting a manicured hand to touch his arm. "She's not your type, King. Newsflash, she belongs in City Hall, and you're a biker."

King jerked away from her touch, his glare turning ice-cold. "Jesus Christ. You're the one who slashed my tire, aren't you? I don't know how I didn't put that together at the time. I should have known."

"You can't prove anything, King."

He took a threatening step toward her. "You have three seconds to tell me where she is."

Janelle scoffed, tilting her head arrogantly. "And if I don't?"

King took a slow, deliberate step toward her, towering over her with barely restrained fury. "Then I stop asking nicely."

Janelle's glare faltered, but she crossed her arms over her chest. "I don't know what you're talking about."

King let out a sharp breath through his nose, his temper flaring hotter. "Last chance, Janelle."

Janelle squared her shoulders. "Or what? You're going to threaten me? Hurt me?"

"I don't hurt women," he growled, his voice deadly quiet. "But I swear to God, if something happens to Ella because of you, I *will* make an exception."

Janelle let out a sharp, humorless laugh. "You're so pathetic," she spat. "Losing your damn mind over some needy—"

King snapped.

His voice boomed through the night. "Where the fuck is she, Janelle?"

Janelle jumped, eyes wide for a split second before she masked it with an evil grin that made him want to vomit.

"So testy. You're kind of hot when you get all angry like this."

Just as he was about to truly lose it on her, a commotion coming toward them caught his attention, and his heart nearly pounded right out of his chest at the sight of it.

TWENTY-SEVEN
ELLA

Ella's voice was hoarse from yelling, but she refused to stop.

She pounded on the locked door, her palms stinging, her breath coming in fast, ragged gasps. "Somebody!" she screamed. "Help! Please!"

Her ankle throbbed painfully, but she didn't care. Fear clawed at her chest. She had no phone, no way to get out, and no idea if anyone could hear her.

But as panic threatened to swallow her whole, the lock clicked.

The door swung open so fast she nearly stumbled.

Kade stood in the doorway, his sharp gaze scanning her frantically before stepping inside and reaching for her.

Remi, wide-eyed, stood behind him. "Oh my gosh, are you okay?"

Ella sucked in a deep, shuddering breath and limped forward, clutching the doorframe. Her body ached, but none of that mattered.

She searched past them wildly, looking for one person and one person only.

Janelle.

"What happened?" Remi asked, stepping closer.

Ella barely registered the question, still scanning the hallway. "It was her," she seethed. "Janelle."

Kade's expression darkened instantly. "What?"

"She—she pushed me in here. Locked me in."

Remi gasped, her hands flying over her mouth. "That bitch."

But Ella was done talking.

Without another word, she stormed forward, ignoring the sharp pain in her ankle.

"Ella, wait—your foot—" Kade started, but she didn't stop.

Nothing could stop her.

She charged toward the front of the clubhouse, fury pounding through her veins. She could hear King shouting from outside when she reached the exit.

A crowd had gathered, whispers buzzing, Daddies standing in a protective semi-circle while Littles peered around them curiously.

And there she was.

Janelle.

Ella saw red.

That bitch was *dead*.

Before anyone could stop her, she lunged.

Janelle barely had time to turn before Ella tackled her.

"You stupid, conniving bitch!" Ella screamed as she grabbed the woman by the hair.

Janelle shrieked, stumbling back as Ella attacked, fists flying.

"I don't care how pretty you think you are. You do not mess with a New York girl, and you especially don't mess with my man!"

The Littles cheered.

"Get her, Ella!" Remi shrieked.

"Rip her hair out!" Ivy added.

"Bite her!" Carlee screamed. "Actually, don't, she probably has rabies."

Janelle shrieked like a dying cat, flailing her arms as she fake-cried. "Someone get her off me!"

Strong arms suddenly wrapped around Ella's waist, lifting her clean off the ground.

Ella kicked wildly as King pulled her back against his chest. "Let me go! I'm not done kicking her ass," she snarled, her entire body vibrating with rage.

King held firm, murmuring low against her ear, "I've got you, baby, I've got you. She's not worth it."

Janelle collapsed onto the ground in a dramatic heap, clutching her face. "She attacked me," she screeched, fake tears spilling down her cheeks. "I was just talking to King—"

"Cut the bullshit, Janelle," Steele growled.

She turned her watery eyes on him, sniffling. "You saw what she did—"

Steele scoffed. "You locked Ella in a room, assaulted her, and trespassed on our property after being warned to stay away." He tilted his head toward the gate. "The cops will be here in five minutes."

Janelle froze.

Then, her face twisted. "You called the cops?"

King's grip on Ella tightened as he stepped forward. "I should've done it the first time you showed up at the firehouse."

Janelle's fake tears disappeared instantly.

"You're making a mistake, King," she hissed.

King scowled. "No, my only mistake was giving you the time of day."

Janelle let out a frustrated scream as sirens filled the air.

Still fuming in King's arms, Ella watched with satisfaction as Steele and Kade stepped forward, ready to hand Janelle over.

As the flashing red-and-blue lights flooded the compound, Ella flipped her off just for fun before King carried her inside.

Ella sat on the clubhouse couch with her arms crossed over her chest, her bottom lip sticking out in a deep pout as Doc kneeled in front of her, gently pressing his fingers around her swollen, painful ankle.

"Owwie!" she yelped dramatically, pulling her leg back.

Doc sighed. "I barely touched you, troublemaker."

"I know," she whined, turning to King, who had her on his lap. "But I hate this."

King arched a brow, his voice low and firm. "You're gonna sit there and let Doc do his job, Little one."

Ella huffed. "But I'm finnnne."

Doc snorted as he pressed gently on the side of her ankle, making her flinch. "Yeah, totally fine," he said dryly. "You twisted it pretty good, Ella. Let me wrap it, or it'll hurt even worse tomorrow."

Ella whined again and looked to King for sympathy.

King wasn't having it.

He leaned in slightly, his voice dropping into a quiet threat. "Keep fussing, baby, and I swear I'll make sure you're in bed all day with no candy salad and no playtime."

Ella's eyes widened. "You wouldn't."

King arched an eyebrow. "Try me."

Her pout deepened, but she huffed and reluctantly let Doc wrap her ankle.

"Good girl," King murmured, his fingers brushing over her neck approvingly.

When Doc finished, he reached into his bag and pulled out a giant, brightly colored lollipop. "For being a *mostly* good patient," he said, handing it to her.

Ella beamed, instantly forgetting her annoyance. "Ooooh! Thank you, Doc!"

Doc rolled his eyes but smiled as he stood. "Now, here's the deal," he said, looking between her and King. "Stay off that foot for at least three days. No walking, running around, or putting weight on it—nothing."

Ella groaned loudly. "*Three* days?"

King, on the other hand, looked completely unbothered. In fact, he looked downright pleased. "You got it, Doc," he said smugly. "She won't lift a finger."

Ella's eyes widened. "Wait—what?"

"You heard the man." King smiled, easily lifting her into his arms. "You're officially on bed rest, Little one."

Ella squeaked as he carried her toward their apartment, a sinking feeling settling in her stomach.

By the second day, Ella was dying from sheer boredom.

King had turned into Mr. Bossy-pants.

She couldn't walk, she couldn't use the toilet alone, she couldn't help clean up after the party, and worst of all—she couldn't get her own juice box.

"Daddy," she whined dramatically from the couch, where she was bundled up like a burrito in an obscene amount of blankets. "I *hate* this."

King, who was casually leaning against the counter, watching her with far too much amusement, took a slow sip of his coffee. "I *love* this," he countered, smirking behind the rim of his mug.

Ella narrowed her eyes, unimpressed. "You're the worst."

"And yet, I'm the one making sure you heal."

Ella huffed, flopping against the pillows with all the grace of a disgruntled toddler. "You're a meanie."

King chuckled, completely unaffected. "I'm a Daddy."

"Same thing," she grumbled, crossing her arms.

Luckily, the Littles had taken pity on her and kept her entertained.

Remi and Carlee brought over a mountain of coloring books and crayons and spent half the afternoon coloring with her.

Harper and Ivy spent hours doing puzzles with her.

Molly read her a story out loud, complete with silly voices, which was adorable.

By the third day, she was still miserable about being stuck inside, but at least she wasn't completely bored.

The only problem?

King was taking Doc's orders *way* too seriously.

"Baby, I swear to God—don't move."

Ella froze mid-scoot, her attempt to sneak off the couch immediately abandoned.

"I wasn't moving," she lied.

King raised a brow from across the room. "Then why do you look guilty?"

"I always look guilty."

King sighed, pinching the bridge of his nose. "What do you need, Little one?"

She perked up immediately as she answered, "Chocolate milk."

"Say please."

Ella batted her lashes. "Please, Daddy."

He shook his head, chuckling as he grabbed a bottle from the fridge. As he walked over to her, he grumbled, "Bossiest Little girl in the world."

Ella beamed, reaching for the bottle. "That's rich coming from the *bossiest* Daddy in the world."

King handed it to her before leaning down and pressing a firm kiss to her forehead. "Damn right."

And even though she pouted every single time he made her rest...

She secretly loved every second of it.

TWENTY-EIGHT
KING

From the moment Doc told Ella she had to stay off her foot, King knew that she was going to be the worst patient in the world.

And he was absolutely right.

As soon as he set her up on the couch with blankets, snacks, and a steady stream of entertainment, she turned into a menace.

"Daddy," she whined dramatically, tilting her head over the arm of the couch. "I need juice."

King looked up from his spot in the kitchen, where he was already pouring her a sippy cup. "I know, baby. That's why I'm getting it."

"But I need it now," she moaned.

King smirked, walking over and handing her the cup. "You're so patient, Little one."

She grinned sweetly. "I know."

An hour later, she was trying to sneak off the couch again.

"*Dollface*," King warned, arms crossed as he watched her shimmy toward the edge of the cushions.

"I wasn't doing anything," she said, freezing mid-scoot.

"Back up," he ordered, pointing at her pile of pillows.

Ella huffed. "You are the most controlling Daddy ever."

King chuckled. "And you are the most impossible Little girl."

By the end of the second day, she had completely given up behaving.

"Daddy," she whined, grabbing his sleeve dramatically. "I can't do this anymore."

He raised a brow. "Do what, baby? Sit on the couch and eat snacks while you watch cartoons?"

She groaned, throwing her head back. "I need to move."

King, amused as hell, casually took another bite of his sandwich. "You can wiggle your fingers."

Ella shot him a glare. "I don't like you very much right now."

King leaned down, pressing a kiss to her forehead. "Yes, you do."

She sighed dramatically. "Fine, I do. But you're still mean."

That was fine. He'd be mean if it meant taking care of his girl.

On the fourth day, when Doc cleared her to walk again, Ella practically leaped off the couch and nearly gave King a heart attack.

"Finally," she squealed. "I survived."

King chuckled, catching her easily. "I told you it wasn't the end of the world."

"It was, but I made it through."

To celebrate, King took her on a day date—just the two of them.

They got ice cream first because King had quickly learned that Ella's love language was sugar.

She got the most ridiculous combination of flavors—cotton candy and mint chocolate chip—while King stuck to good old-fashioned chocolate.

When she tried to steal a bite of his, he raised a brow but

gave her a taste because he couldn't seem to say no to her unless it was about her health or safety.

After ice cream, they went to the aquarium, where Ella pressed her face against the glass of every single exhibit like an excited child and tried to talk to all the animals.

"Oh my gosh," she gasped, grabbing King's arm. "Look at his little face."

He glanced at the fish in question. "Baby, that thing is ugly."

Ella turned and smacked his arm. "He's precious!"

King laughed, wrapping an arm around her waist. "You're precious."

That evening, they met her parents for dinner at the steakhouse in town.

Even in a restaurant, King couldn't stop taking care of her. He just did it in a way that was less obvious.

He cut her steak into small pieces without her asking. He handed her a napkin before she even knew she needed one. When she reached for her drink, he automatically tilted the straw toward her mouth.

She giggled and blushed. "You're so ridiculous."

King winked at her. "You love it."

Halfway through the meal, her parents exchanged a look before her mom cleared her throat. "So, Ella," she started, smiling. "We have some news."

He was pretty sure he already knew what it was, but Ella had no clue.

Ella perked up. "What is it?"

Her dad grinned. "We bought a house."

Ella blinked. "In New York?"

"Here. In Shadowridge," her mom announced, clapping her hands together.

Ella froze.

King beamed.

Her father chuckled. "We've been working with a real estate agent since we arrived. We'll be splitting our time between here and New York."

Ella gasped so loudly that half the restaurant turned to look at her, but she didn't even notice. "Are you serious?"

Her mom laughed. "Totally serious."

Ella threw her arms around King's neck, squeezing him so tightly he nearly choked. "Did you know about this?"

He shrugged and winked at her.

"Oh my gosh, this is the best day ever," she said as tears filled her eyes.

King chuckled, pressing a kiss to the side of her head. "Just wait, baby. It's about to get better."

After dinner, the two of them walked to a nearby park to get some air before heading home. Ella slipped her hand into King's, squeezing it.

"Thank you," she said. "For everything. My life is *so* much better because of you."

King's heart swelled.

He stopped walking, turning to face her completely.

"I'm glad I changed your life, baby," he said softly. "But there's one more thing I want to change."

Ella frowned slightly. "What do you mean?"

King reached into his pocket, pulling out a small velvet box before dropping to one knee.

Ella's breath caught in her throat.

When he flipped it open, revealing a stunning diamond ring, her hands flew to her mouth.

"I wanna change your last name, Little one."

Ella squeaked. "Are you proposing to me right now?"

King chuckled. "I am. I know it's quick, but I knew you were meant to be mine the second I met you. I want to give you everything you've always dreamed of. You make me so happy, and I want to spend the rest of my life as your husband and Daddy. Will you marry me, dollface?"

Ella launched herself at him, knocking him backward onto the grass. "Yes!"

King laughed as she peppered kisses all over his face.

Right then, King knew he was truly the luckiest man in the world.

ALSO BY KATE OLIVER

Syndicate Kings

Corrupting Cali: Declan's Story

Saving Scarlet: Killian's Story

Controlling Chloe: Bash's Story

Possessing Paisley: Kieran's Story

Keeping Katie: Grady's Story

Taking Tessa: Ronan's Story

Daddies of Pine Hollow

Jaxon

Dane

Nash

Dark Ops Daddies

Cage

Jasper

Savage Sins

Savage Revenge

KEEP UP WITH KATE!

Sign up for my newsletter get teasers, cover reveals, updates, and extra content!

SCAN ME TO SIGN UP NOW!

The kindest thing you can do for an author is to leave a positive review!

Printed in Great Britain
by Amazon

59490573R00119